Sheila began her career as a nurse then health visitor before completing a degree and becoming a teacher. She taught in a range of settings but quickly began to work with children in care, either in schools or at local authority level. Working with children in care, Sheila developed a deep understanding of the struggles they, and other vulnerable children and young people, experience. Currently she trains teachers and other professionals in ways to support vulnerable students.

Sheila has written a book for teachers, *Overcoming Barriers to Learning,* and a book about mindset, *Make it Magnificent.*

For children and young people everywhere who all deserve to grow up surrounded by love.

Sheila Mulvenney

FIVE DAYS IN FEBRUARY

AUSTIN MACAULEY PUBLISHERS™

LONDON • CAMBRIDGE • NEW YORK • SHARJAH

A CIP catalogue record for this title is available from the British Library.

ISBN 9781035838257 (Paperback)
ISBN 9781035838264 (ePub e-book)

www.austinmacauley.com

First Published 2024
Austin Macauley Publishers Ltd®
1 Canada Square
Canary Wharf
London
E14 5AA

Prologue

It's funny how I can remember some of the tiny details of that first time I met him. How cold it was; the fact that the heavy frost sparkled and 'crunched' as I walked on it. The way I drew a sharp breath in from the shock of seeing him there, and how that breath felt cold going through my nose and down the back of my throat, spreading inside me. How he looked young and innocent and somehow small, though when he stood, I had to look up at him.

Yet, many of the details of events that followed in the next few days blur in my mind; like looking through a steamed up window, I want to wipe a clear patch. Of course, I had to go over it lots, with the police and my parents, so I must know the details somewhere in my brain. Perhaps the first time I met him is clear because I am looking for clues.

Something that would have given me a hint at what was to follow, then I would have done things differently. I would, wouldn't I?

It was my counsellor's idea. She said I should simply start at the beginning and write it all down. I have been seeing her for several months now. Well, seeing isn't the right word, I mean I do see her but it's a talking cure really. I have been talking with her? At her maybe? I think she is supposed to help me get a better perspective on events. Put them in proportion I suppose.

After it all happened, I just sort of withdrew. Shame and guilt can do that to you. Well, they did that to me.

I think what she has been trying to do is make me feel less guilty. But I don't want that. Surely, sometimes there can be a righteous guilt? Not everything was my fault. I can see that. I could do that on my own. I really didn't need a counsellor to tell me that. But I also know that quite a lot of what happened was my fault.

She says I need to learn to take responsibility just for those things and not feel that everything that happened was down to me and what I did. But what I've been wondering is who is responsible for the very last ripple in the pond. Is it the person who threw the pebble into the still deep water? The person who first broke that flat shiny surface? Or at some point is that person relieved of responsibility for what the pebble itself causes? I don't have an answer…yet!

That is why she thought I should write it all down. She must think it's a good plan because she said she won't see me any more till I've done it. Or maybe she's just bored with our Wednesday afternoon sessions. Maybe she'd rather meet a mate on a Wednesday at 3pm for a glass of wine or a cappuccino, or maybe even meet a lover. Or perhaps she's spotted a Pilates class she'd like to go to instead.

Don't get me wrong, she is perfectly nice and she makes hot chocolate for me. Not sure which counselling theory that comes from. Freudian?—Oh no! I'm not going there! I think she just does it to 'relax' me. We do the pleasantries while she makes it before we get down to the real hard work of analysis, or reflection, or whatever.

One thing about going to see her is it has made me do quite a bit of research about counselling. She is broadly humanistic in her approach but with a NLP bias (neurolinguistic programming for those who haven't really explored the world of counselling). I think it means kind of re-programming certain thought pathways.

Her name is Marcia Marchant. I couldn't help myself from telling her she sounded like a heroine from a Bronte novel. I go to her home which seems odd to me. I mean boundaries! What if I really was, or scarier still, evolving into a nutcase. I know where she lives. Seems kind of careless to me!

She sees me in the front lounge of a small terraced house. It has Georgian windows, a white picket fence and although, it is slap bang in the middle of town, it gives the appearance of a little cottage. The room is lined with books and the sofas are cream. Counselling is clearly not messy, judging by the spotless cream sofas. No mess in this counsellor's front room, that's for sure.

Although, I have counted three separate boxes of tissues in the room. To mop up the emotional messes of her counselees I guess. Good thing tears are colourless. Imagine, if tears were chocolate coloured! I bet she wouldn't have cream sofas then.

It is just possible that I am now indulging in a displacement activity. Prattling on about my counselling instead of beginning to tell you my story. So I guess I'd better stop here and get on with the real business, and tell you what happened during those few short days, and how several lives were changed forever.

Chapter 1

The morning I first met Seb, it was cold, very cold. I lay in bed, in my dressing gown and thick socks—a must in our house in winter. It was an old Victorian house and my parents had lovingly 'restored' it, which meant putting in lots of fireplaces and repairing architrave but hadn't extended to replacing the very old sash windows.

Authentic, yes, but they let an icy gale blow through, despite the very heavy, lined, curtain which was supposed to shield my slumbering form from the icy onslaught. It failed, hence dressing gown, with several layers underneath, and hot water bottle (always cold of course by morning) were obligatory all winter.

It was a Saturday and I gingerly put a hand out of the covers to pull back the curtain and peek outside. It was white with a thick frost. Pretty, but I had to be at ballet in an hour. I suppose I do need to fill you in on a few details about myself. I was 17, and in the lower sixth form at the local school. I didn't want to be. I wanted to go to musical theatre college but my parents persuaded me to stay on and get 'A' levels and then audition for musical theatre college.

I hadn't really enjoyed it so far. I was doing drama and art, sociology (goodness knows why), and of course, dance.

Thing is, the dance at school is more about analysing it and choreography, and any dance that we actually 'do' is contemporary which is my least favourite. It always seems to involve rolling around on the floor, which frankly, I just don't see as dance.

What I like is theatre dance, you know tap and ballet and modern and jazz. In my mind, you just can't beat some of the dance routines in musicals—like the tap dancing in *42nd Street*—all those feet somehow tapping in rhythm at the exact same time or the energetic dancing of *Footloose*, or, one of my favourites, the dancing story to 'I didn't do it' in *Chicago*. Now that is dancing.

But on Saturdays, I get to continue with what I call my proper dancing—ballet at 8.30, then tap and modern, and finally an hour of pointe practice. Oh joy! So, frost or no frost, I got into my leotard, pulled on some jazz trousers over the top, then grabbed my ski jacket from my wardrobe. I had only ever been skiing once, in year ten, but I have had so much use out of ski jacket every winter since then, the price per wear has plummeted!

Our house is one of those long thin houses that begins at the road, with a tiny front garden, then stretches back for miles. As you go in from the front, there is a lounge (with open fire of course) then another lounge. We call it the music room because it is where dad plays piano and guitar and any other instrument he seems able to get his hands on.

Then the stairs go up on the right and on the left, there is a huge cloakroom—quite definitely a room—then a breakfast room (which we use as a posh dining room—so we hardly ever use it), then a huge kitchen and breakfast room with French windows onto the back garden, which then stretches further still and has 2 huge pear trees, an apple tree and a huge holly tree.

At Christmas, the whole street gets holly from our tree. There is also a shed full of various tools and there is still my old wooden 'Wendy house'. Each summer, dad says we must take it down as he fancies a pond there but somehow it is still there. There are also no end of deceased pets buried in the garden—2 goldfishes, 3 hamsters, 2 guinea pigs, 2 rabbits and 1 cat.

At the end of the garden, there is a lane that sort of leads nowhere but means that folk who have built garages in their back gardens can actually get their cars into them. Upstairs is pretty huge too. My bedroom is at the back and it is enormous—definitely the envy of most of my friends. Mum and dad's room is at the front and in between there is a study and a guest bedroom and a huge family bathroom.

My own personal view is that we should move the study and put an ensuite there for me but I am still working on persuading mum and dad about that.

I went downstairs that morning and knew dad would still be in bed and mum probably out at the gym. I grabbed a quick bowl of cereal, which I ate standing up in the kitchen, then went out the back door as the back lane was the quickest route to my dance school. Just before I went out, I grabbed a banana and apple out of the fruit bowl—three hours of dancing is very tiring but I am always trying to watch my weight; leotards hide nothing!

I was walking through the garden when I noticed the door of the Wendy house open. Our cat, Tigger, is known to get herself stuck in neighbour's garages, or cars, if she finds herself near an open door for more than a few minutes. So, I thought I ought to check she hadn't got in there rather than just shut the door. I was always surprised by how far I had to duck down to get in it.

When I used it as a small child, I had curtains which were left shut, so although it was really bright outside, it was dark inside. I sort of stooped at the door with my head inside calling 'Tigger'. Not that she ever comes to being called so I reached in with a hand and grabbed one of the very old musty bean bags which had been left in there and dragged it forward while glancing around.

My heart skipped as I was aware of a movement in the far corner but it was a bigger movement than a cat. The other bean bag moved, my heart practically stopped and I saw the shape of young lad sit up. I was ready to duck back outside but his face, as he opened his eyes, looked young—and frightened. Like a rabbit in headlights.

I bent down onto one knee. "Are you OK?" I asked. I was aware my voice sounded normal but inside my heart was racing.

He sat up straighter. "Bloody freezing actually!"

"But what are you doing here?"

"Well, I was sleeping, or trying to! It is really hard to sleep when you're bloody freezing."

"But…I mean, where should you be. Won't you're parents be worried sick about you?"

I noticed he had really broad shoulders and was quite overweight but his face was definitely quite childlike.

"I live at the children's home."

"The one by the supermarket?" It was quite well known in the area but of course we were all warned to stay away from it.

He nodded.

"Well, I'm sure they will be worried anyway?"

"They." He really emphasised the word. "Will have reported me missing last night to the police but that's where it will end. Fresh shift this morning, they will have to phone the police and their supervisors when I turn up. I certainly won't get my points again this week."

"You've done this before then?"

"Maybe."

"Have you slept here before?"

"Maybe. There aren't too many places around here that are open for folk like me."

"I thought there was a hostel up the road?"

"It's only for grown-ups—'minors'." He used his fingers to make sort of speech marks around the word. "Get returned to their parents or in my case 'the home'." Fingers again. "I have tried."

"Look, do you want to come inside and have some breakfast?"

What was I thinking? I had ballet, some sort of rational voice inside me was saying.

"No, thanks, I'll head back to the home—it'll be OK."

"Is there something wrong there—are you mistreated or something…"

"Oh, spare me please," he said with an impression of pretentious pity. "Like you care anyway."

He moved towards the door so I retreated as gracefully as it is possible to from a Wendy house when you are 5'8" and the doorway is designed for a child of 3. I was expecting he'd say something, or talk or even hit me I guess, but then he just stepped past me, stretched and I noticed that he must have

Well, obviously, I have to tell you a bit about Tess and Josh. Tess is one of my very best mates. She goes to the same school and we became mates in year seven. We haven't seen quite so much of each other lately as she is going out with Jack and it all seems to have got a bit intense but we still get on great.

I think I am a bit of a disappointment to her as she'd like me to go out with one of Jack's mates so we can do couple sort of things, which I think Tess sees as being kind of 'mature'. Josh is in year thirteen same as Jack but Josh happens to be absolutely gorgeous. Just to be clear here, we are talking Ashton Kutcher kind of gorgeous.

Sadly, I am not the only one who thinks so and for ages, he was simply off limits as he was going out with Olivia, also in year thirteen, but they broke up in the autumn. Ripples of excitement went around the girl population of the school when we found out. For a time, I must confess, I thought I was in with a bit of a chance.

I'd never really chatted to him much before but then he joined our sociology group—he was in the year above but had decided to do an extra AS in year thirteen; well, I for one approved of his choice. We didn't really chat a lot in class but at least he then knew I existed and would even acknowledge me in school if we passed in the corridor or happened to be in the common room at the same time.

Then another stroke of luck happened. I was doing some extra musical theatre exams (Trinity) through school and my classes were on a Wednesday after school. It did involve a lot of work. I had to do various monologues, one from *Lady Windermere's Fan*, one from *Dear Nobody* (I even had to have a pregnancy testing kit for that which caused great parental hilarity, of the cringing kind, at my expense).

I also had to do a song and dance routine from *Anything Goes* and a song from *Les Miserable*. But luckily, my lessons just happened to be at the time that he had guitar lessons, so often we would end up chatting while we waited. Better yet, there was just the two of us and both Miss Brown and Mr Hanson were often late.

We seemed to get along really well and for a time, I had even managed to delude myself that he might ask me out. Then he just seemed to drop me, though he did send me a couple of really cryptic texts saying he hoped I was OK and that everything would work out for me. At the time I did reply, sort of vaguely, because I didn't know what he was on about.

But then I sat my Trinity exams, and sadly, only saw him in sociology lessons when he smiled but seemed to keep me at arm's length. Of course, Tess knew how much I fancied him and was often trying to engineer times when we might end up at the same get together, etc., despite me telling her often that she was wasting her time as he obviously wasn't interested or I had upset him or something, or maybe I had just imagined, in a sad 'stalky' way that he'd been quite friendly for a time.

On that Saturday, I met Tess in Costa. There are lots of really frustrating things about living in a small town but one of the good things—can't think of any other good points about Blythton just now—is that almost everywhere is walking distance from almost everywhere else. Just as well really as I must say the bus service is crap and I haven't sat my test yet.

We drank hot chocolates with cream on top and marshmallows. She then proceeded to tell me that Rashida (best friend of Olivia, Josh's ex) had told Rebecca (friend of Tess' older sister, Maddy) who then told Maddy that Olivia had asked Josh if there was anyone he was seeing (to be truthful, she probably wanted him to say that he was still hopelessly in love with her but if she did, then it backfired 'ha bloomin ha') because he said that there was someone he was hoping to ask out if he hadn't already messed it up.

"So!" was my considered reply to this excitedly imparted information, of little consequence it seemed to me.

"But it might be you—he might have been secretly admiring you from afar for ages, and it sounds like he knows he's been an idiot in sort of giving you the cold shoulder treatment."

There are lots of really irritating things about Tess (though outweighed by the fact that she is lovely and brilliant and my best mate), one of them being that if she wants something to happen (me going out with one of Jack's mates for instance), she just assumes it will happen and in her mind makes everything else that happens be a source of 'evidence' or mystic sign for what she believes is some cosmic movement towards her desired outcome.

I sighed. "Oh, Tess! First, can we really believe, or count as accurate in any way, something that Olivia told Rashida who told Maddy who told you?" Some people have been known to say I can be a bit of pedantic. "Secondly, the fact that he may want to go out with someone does not provide any evidence that someone could possibly be me—remember about 250 girls, in our school alone, fancy him."

"Yeah, but you are gorgeous!"

"Yeah, but you are my best friend!"

"Yeah, but he is coming to the party tonight and Jack (said with emphasis to somehow imply his reliability as a source) told me that he asked specifically if you were going to be there."

That did it; my cool, nonchalant, exterior vanished, my heart started to speed up and I burbled. "Did he? Really?" I stuttered.

Which took great effort as my brain and mouth seemed to be very far away from each other suddenly, which made any sort of speech difficult. I have often thought it is strange that when you really like someone, your body seems to try it's hardest to make you look especially unattractive—face goes red, you sweat, become incoherent to mention but a few of the unattractive features.

I thought 'nature' was meant to help out with this sort of thing—survival of the race, etc.—so much for biological theories.

"I thought he was meant to be away this weekend or something. Oh my God! What am I going to wear?" I burbled.

That's another funny thing. I had been really looking forward to the party tonight but now it felt like a big panic, because clearly I had to look 'hot'. I was, at the same time, really glad he was going—what's a little pressure about how you look matter when dream boat (plus lots of other 'fit' girls who look much more gorgeous than me) will be there.

"Well, let's get shopping then," came my supportive mate's solution to my 'outfit to pull fit guy' wardrobe dilemma.

The afternoon passed quickly as we browsed and bought and bumped into various other mates. Tess was staying round mine after the party but we each headed to our homes for tea and she was going to come round about 7.30 so we could get ready together, which means trying on a least half a dozen outfits before finally settling on the first one, then leaving all the others are in a big sprawling mess on the floor, so that finding space to put up the camp bed in my room becomes a serious challenge.

I had a shower when I got in, then headed down when dad shouted that tea was ready. It was lasagne, one of my favourites, and I must say dad does a mean lasagne.

When I was in the shower, I had decided that I would tell mum and dad about the boy in the Wendy house. I had always planned to but unless I'd woken dad up AND made myself very late, there seemed no point doing it that morning. After all, he had left, so no harm done.

I was surprised mum wasn't in when I sat down at the table, the smell of the lasagne, with garlic bread and salad was really tempting my taste buds.

I was just having a garlic bread debate in my head (which went something like 'Go on, have some you know you love it. Yes, but you are going to a party and the boy of your dreams will be there so you want to look hot. You know you have danced a lot today. People pull at parties; you do need to look super-hot tonight. Dad will wonder what's up if you refuse it.') when mum came through the front door.

Dad put down the garlic bread which he had just been bringing to the table and gave her a hug. I guess he must have known she'd had a tough day. He handed her a glass of wine (I am really not to blame for any alcoholic tendencies I may have or may yet develop—blame the parents I say). Mum just sank into the chair. I do mean sank. It was like whatever had been holding her up—some hook from the ceiling—just gave way.

I felt I was the outsider, so as dad shared out the lasagne, I ventured, "Tough day I guess."

"Oh, honey, I really ought to be used to it by now but it still gets to me."

Friends at school tell me I am not always good on tact with my size 7 feet, I asked, "What does?"

"Two sisters taken into care. I had to take them in with the clothes they stood up in from the police station they'd spent the early morning at when they'd been collected from. Well, anyway, and then drive them to Norfolk to a women they've never met before and say 'this is where you'll be staying—bye now—not sure when you'll see your dad again, not sure what life will be like for you now.'

"Oh, but I do know that proportionally kids that grow up in care do less well in almost every measurable *outcome* than their peers' (she was visibly cross when she spat out these words).You should have seen their faces; the little one's lip was quivering and her big sis kept putting her arm round her and saying it would be OK and not to worry."

"But why?" *Just dig deeper why don't you*, some inner voice challenged but I ignored it. I should have just eaten the lasagne and shut my mouth.

"Their mum was an alcoholic—though she herself had been physically abused by her mum—who is still alive and I believe one of the most vicious women on earth. Well, their mum died about 2 years ago—a liver can only take so much…" Mum laughed as she took a sip of her wine.

"Their dad has a long history of mental illness; he was in a psychiatric unit for years when he was younger and I think he does try but he just doesn't cope, so after numerous feuds with neighbours and unpaid bills, he was evicted. Someone put a call through to the office this morning when they found them and several suitcases and carrier bags in a shop doorway; they had been there all night.

"Their dad was passed out cold. He'd had a lot of cider and I guess with the tablets he's probably on, it wasn't a good mix. In fact, passed out is mild, practically comatose I think. He'd thrown up and the two girls had just sort of shuffled down to his feet and were simply frozen and hugging each other and crying. So…"

She went on having another gulp of wine and taking a deep breath in, said, "At least they will be in a warm bed tonight."

Dad sort of broke the silence that followed by making some banal comment about the lasagne getting cold and it worked and we ate while chatting about superficial pleasantries—the way dad insisted on using the cracked dish for lasagne and mum was convinced that one day the lasagne would escape before it got to the table, and the fact that Martha and her family who lived three doors up the street had apparently got all their visas and would be off to Australia for a new life in a just a few weeks.

I enjoyed the food but I didn't mention the boy in the Wendy house—I just kept wishing I would hear the doorbell that signalled Tess' arrival. Which sure enough, eventually, I didn't waste any time leaving the table.

Chapter 3

Getting ready consisted of a lot of larking about, singing a little too loudly to Lady Gaga, Adele, Rita Ora and Nicki Minaj, trying on far too many outfits, which were then discarded on to the floor, practising sexy dance moves which really weren't very sexy at all—the usual girls sort of stuff.

When we went downstairs to leave, mum was there and she seemed in a good mood (me thinks perhaps the wine helped), telling us to make sure we had a good time—we were only going to be young once! She was definitely mellow if not tipsy but she stressed at making sure we shared the taxi home—obviously, as we were both coming back here to sleep.

What is it about parents that seem to want to tell you about stuff that is obvious? But then, she redeemed herself by telling us how gorgeous we looked—trust me no girl ever, ever, tires of hearing that she looks good—even if she knows it's not true, she will enjoy hearing it. It is simply a fact of life.

When we walked into Tia's house, we were fashionably late. It was heaving and the atmosphere was heavy with smoke, of one sort or another. We saw a few mates and went to chat to them, then Tess saw Jack and she went over to him but I was nicely ensconced with a group of mates and a Bacardi breezer by then, so that was fine.

I have to confess I had done a quick sweep of the room and no sign of Josh—obviously I wasn't really looking, you know, but of course there were folks in the kitchen and in the garden, despite what had felt like sub-zero temperatures on the way over to the party. I was having a good time, but then I saw him—he had just come through from the other room and he did look straight at me—honest I really didn't imagine that.

He smiled, and have I ever mentioned that when Josh smiles, he has this really lovely wide mouth and his nose kind of crinkles and his eyes sort of…twinkle.

Anyway, he took a slug from the bottle of whatever he was holding and sort of motioned for me to come over. I got up from the bean bag I was sitting on—probably not as elegantly as I might but bean bags are tricky things, especially when wearing quite a short denim skirt.

"So," he said when I reached him, "how did you get on with those exams you were doing?"

"Fine! Actually, I got a distinction." Not cool! I know, in fact it made me sound sort of geeky but it just came out!

"Well done you then. I haven't seen you much since then."

"I know it seemed, if I'm honest, like you were …avoiding me a bit."

He smiled again. "No! It's just…look I'll explain all that later. I missed our chats though."

"Me too," I said this looking right at him because this article in *Closer* said eye contact was one of the ways you could show a guy you fancied him. I smiled at him as well, just for good measure.

Then we just went on chatting. It was great; he made me laugh and even though my heart was racing and my tummy turning somersaults, I felt kind of relaxed. I told him all sorts of stuff about me and what I wanted to do and what I liked.

We were standing between the kitchen and lounge, and at one point, someone wanted to get past and he just sort of put his hand on my shoulder and pulled me to him. Sigh! There was literally a hairs breadth between our faces and he looked into my eyes and just smiled. Later, some of his beer sort of dribbled onto my arm when someone knocked him and he sort of wiped it away with his fingers and it made me tingle.

All too soon he said he had to go because he was giving Tony a lift and he had to be home early as he had a football match in the morning. But he asked if we could meet up the next day and maybe go for a walk or something. I said yes that was fine, trying to sound casual and hesitating bit—like I might have had to consider if I was free, in a desperate attempt not to sound too desperate!

He said he would text me, then he just sort of leaned over and I couldn't really say he kissed me—I wanted him too, heck yes, I did—but he just sort of let his lips touch mine. Oh heaven. Then he left. Well, when I managed to get myself down from the cloud I felt I was on, which was due solely to him rather than any plant derivative that might have been floating in the air, I wanted to just go home.

It felt that the magic bubble might burst if I stayed. But I sort of had to stay. Tess was, well, I don't know where Tess was but I suspected upstairs somewhere with Jack.

Somehow it got to taxi time. Tess didn't want to go home. She had drunk a bit too much, as is usual for her at parties. I felt high as a kite but it really wasn't alcohol. I was dying to tell Tess all about Josh but I knew she would conk out as soon as we got home. She was a bit loud when we were going in the house and I kept trying to shush her but she just kept copying me saying 'shush' too loudly and putting her finger to her lips, then starting to giggle and chat really loudly again.

I was trying to be quiet but mum came down the stairs just as Tess was saying, "Sorry but I can't get up them, they are sooo high," as she sat on the third stair.

Thank goodness for mums. I knew it was OK as mum was smiling when she appeared on the stairs.

"Need a hand, girls?" She asked but didn't really wait for an answer. She sort of helped Tess into the room (and this was surprising. Somehow all the discarded clothes were in neat piles and the spare bed was up; mums eh? Where would we be? Unless the room tidying fairy I had wished for half my life had finally decided to put in an appearance, but I suspect not).

Mum asked if I was OK. She told me to wake her if Tess was ill but as expected, as soon as Tess' head hit the pillow, before mum had even left the room, she started breathing heavily, if not quite snoring. Mum hugged and kissed me goodnight saying she hoped it had been a good night.

It was about half past five when I woke. I don't know what woke me. But as soon as I was awake, my mind filled with warm soppy thoughts about the lovely Josh and the fact that he was going to text me today and we were going to meet up. I was lying in my bed but I knew I had this big grin on my face.

Tess was breathing heavily on the bed next to mine. I was warm and cosy in my bed but I could feel the icy draught coming in through my window when I put my hand up to it.

I knew he would be there. I don't know how but I knew without any doubt.

I must just say, I wasn't wild about getting out of my cosy bed to trek outside in the dark and freezing cold but I kind of felt I had to.

I crept downstairs and made 2 mugs of hot chocolate and some peanut butter sandwiches. He was there and whatever instinctive gut intuition thing had happened inside me, it was accurate on this occasion. Surprisingly, he was awake—though I guess that's not surprising really—he had said it was hard to sleep when you are freezing, unless you become hypothermic in which case you may well sleep then die.

OMG, what if? The thought had flashed through my mind while I was making the hot chocolate and it prompted me to have the forethought to take a torch—which I found after a lot of rooting around in the kitchen drawer and I guess he had seen the light as I walked up the garden path (not metaphorically obviously).

I nearly baptised him with hot chocolate as I bent down to get in with torch and sarnies and 2 mugs but he knelt up to take one from me. In different circumstances, it could have been quite the comedy scene—Wendy houses are simply not very big—in fact I wonder how parents manage to get in to sort out the various catastrophes that happen inside them.

"Thanks," he said as I settled myself into the opposite corner and then offered him the sandwiches after grabbing one myself.

We just sat in silence for a few minutes—you have to remember I was still pretty half asleep.

"So, do you come here every night?" I asked.

"NO." He sounded affronted.

"So is it just a phase or something?"

"There's this other kid and he really pisses me off. Winds me up so I just take off because he is such a little runt. If I let myself get cross with him, I would really do some damage."

"Why not tell someone? At the home I mean. Then they could stop him."

"They see it happening but he's such a gobby idiot, he doesn't stop, he just kind of goes on and on—really calm like but needling away. Or, he does it very sneakiretly when no one is able to hear, pisses me right off and I know if he's in that kind of mood, I've got to go to my room or just get out for a bit."

"You mean secretly, or sneakily I guess." I really don't why I corrected him—mispronouncing or even making up new words definitely wasn't his biggest problem right now and it made me sound like a stupid know-it-all. While I was thinking this, I also thought, *What a great word, why on earth isn't it a word?*

"Whatever." He shrugged.

"Why are you in the home, did something happen to your mum and dad?"

"I suppose you could say that."

There was a silence and I thought he wasn't going to tell me and I was just wondering if it would be really bad form to ask another question when he continued.

"I think me mum was a bit…simple. She was OK though. Tiny, in photographs. Dad was a bit of a giant though. That's why I'm so big; I am only 13 you know. I've been this size since I was just over 11! Thing is, everyone seems to expect you to be all 'adult' when you are this size." He used his fingers to put in imaginary parenthesis.

"Anyway, me dad liked his drink and sometimes when he got really drunk, he would lash out a bit. It didn't happen often and mum would make sure me and my sis was in our rooms. Then one night, I guess he thumped her a bit too hard and she never woke up. He went down for it of course. We went to grandma's first—dad's mum.

"My mum never had any folks. She used to say she'd been left on some church steps when she was little and she grew up in a children's home. But grandma was quite old and then we went to foster carers, various different ones, mostly together but sometimes we were split up. Last one we were together though and that was OK till my sister got gobby and she'd stay out all night.

"I know she's a pain but she is my sister, so I was always on her side. Then they said they couldn't cope with us anymore and we came to this home about 2 years ago."

"Oh, so does your sister live there with you?"

He shook his head. "No, only boys in my house—she's in a village—Hortonbrook, I think, part of the same set up. I see her occasionally at sort of joint 'do's and visits and stuff."

"How old is she?"

"She's 15 but she can be a right cow though takes no crap from no one. I think she drives them mad at her home. Always sneaking out coz she's got some boyfriend—I hear the staff talking sometimes."

"I'm sure my mum could help, she's a social worker."

I cringe as I write it what a do goody, stupid know-it-all I must have sounded when I really hadn't got the faintest idea what his life was like.

He rolled his eyes.

"Fucking busy bodies always poking their noses in and messing things up. Guess how many different social workers I've had. Go on guess."

"God, I don't know, 4. No, it's been quite a few years maybe 5 or 6."

"18. NO kidding. 18 bloody social workers. Just don't talk to me about stupid fucking social workers."

He looked quite angry so I thought maybe it was best to let it drop. There was a silence while we each had a mouthful of sandwich and a drink.

"Anyway, I'm Izzy," I said in a formal sort of way and I stuck my hand out towards his. I think maybe I meant it as a joke or maybe I really was just going for the enormous idiot award! "What's your name?"

He shook mine with a sort of 'what a twit we have here' look on his face.

"Seb." He stretched. "Fucking freezing again, isn't it?"

I nodded as I was mid-yawn but couldn't help noticing again how big he was when he stretched.

"You look knackered, you should get back to bed." As he said this, I thought how funny really the whole fact that he was younger and yet telling me what to do and he was right. Also that I had a bed—something I have taken for granted every single night of my life, and grumbled constantly about the cold, which was obviously on a whole different spectrum to the cold of an unheated wooden playhouse in the garden.

But I replied simply, "I was at a party last night and my mate, she's asleep upstairs, got a bit tipsy—surprised you didn't hear her giggling like mad when we got out the taxi."

"Was it good then, the party?"

"Yeah, thanks, yeah it was."

I could feel myself smiling as I remembered just HOW good it was.

"Well, that means there's a lad. I can tell. Just like my sister, you are all soppy over boys. Thing is, when you're all daft and dizzy, you can get taken for a bit of a ride."

How could he know this? He was only 13 and hardly knew me. Even if I was being obvious, he seemed really able to 'see' what I was thinking and his philosophy seemed more in keeping with a middle aged mother cautioning her wayward daughter than a 13 year old boy.

"That's all a bit cynical coming from such a young man." I tried to add emphasis to the word 'man'.

He sighed.

"It's just the way the world is."

Whenever he spoke, he let the words out in quite a deliberate way, like he was either thinking really carefully, or was doing you a huge favour just to talk.

"I might go see my sister today."

"I thought you said she was in Hortonbrook?"

He nodded. "Yup."

"So how on earth are you going to get there? I mean, its Sunday, hardly any buses."

He looked at me like I was his very pathetic, mentally incapable and generally dysfunctional little sister.

"Dooohhh! Hitch."

"But isn't that, you know, sort of dangerous?"

He shook his head.

"Not if you know what you are doing—like me. Obviously, for someone who's been mummy's little darling like you, then yes, it probably would be dangerous."

"What'll you do? Just sort of stroll in and say 'Hi' in the middle of Sunday lunch."

"Well, I will go to the home, then I'll decide at the time— maybe a few stones at the window or a message. I could give to one of the other girls out having a fag or something. Or my sis might come out for a fag, though more often than not she's grounded for something, not that it stops HER getting out."

"Do you get on with her? I mean, can you chat to her and stuff."

"She's my sister!" He said this like I was particularly intellectually challenged.

"I know…it's just….well actually, I don't, I'm an only child. I've always wanted a sister, or a brother, but lots of my friends seem to hate their sisters or brothers. I was just wondering."

"She's OK, Natty is. At least I know she understands all this crap—being in care and stuff."

He looked at me and spoke kind of slowly again.

"If I should happen to be here again and if you happen to bring food again, for which I am extreeemly grateful…" He had an air of grandeur like he was playing a part or rather over playing a part.

"…you ought to know that I love any kind of bread and absolutely any kind of chocolate but I hate fruit except sack sumas."

"Sorry, you mean sat? Satsumas?"

"Don't come all bloody teachery on me…I was just saying for your Hinformation." He over pronounced again.

"Sorry so was I…I just wasn't sure if you were joking or had just you know…thought that…" I could hear myself I just couldn't seem to stop the words dribbling from my mouth.

He stretched.

"Well, I'm going to have to walk somewhere just to warm up."

I yawned. "Yeah, it is freezing."

By the time I had replied, he was standing (well crouched and half way through the door).

He turned back.

"Thanks," he said.

Then he was gone, jogging slowly up our back garden and into the back lane. I realised that I probably had frostbite in my toes which could put to an end to my brilliant career in dance!

Chapter 4

When I crept back into my bed, Tess was still breathing heavily and muttering to herself, or someone, in her sleep. I'd like to say that I sank into the cosy depths of my warm inviting bed, but it would be a lie. Sure enough it was really comfortable and I was so exhausted, my eyes were almost closed.

I pulled my dressing gown tight around me and lay curled on my side with the covers up over my head in the hope I would warm up eventually, but frankly, it didn't seem likely. I tried to think warm thoughts, sun, beaches, real fires, bonfires, hot chocolate, but my head was full of thoughts about Seb and how different his life was and how horrible it would be not to have my own parents, my own house my own room.

But warm thoughts, or sheer exhaustion, must have worked eventually, because when I heard mum coming into the room at about 11.00, I was warm and comfortable and had to drag myself to the surface from a deep and dream free sleep.

"Hi, darlings." She was sort of half whispering. "I brought some breakfast and some painkillers."

She looked at Tess when she said this last bit. Tess was stretching and yawning on the camp bed.

Mum came over to me and kissed me on the cheek—I must confess to surprise. Generally, she is affectionate and loving but kissing me on the cheek in bed in the morning when a friend was staying over was a tad out of the ordinary.

"I'm off to the gym, love. I'll do a proper roast for dinner but not till about two if that's OK?"

I replied sleepily, "Yeah, course that's fine, see you later."

"Oh," I said as an afterthought. "I might be going out later, but I'll say after about three?"

"That's fine, honey, see you later." Mum smiled as she left the room. She looked OK, she just seemed a bit odd. Maybe it was me.

Anyway, I didn't have time to consider it further as Tess shot over to the tray mum had brought and passed me a glass of orange juice.

"Your mum's brill," she said as she stuffed some croissant into her mouth and threw one to me.

I laughed. "How can you possibly NOT feel ill? You drank a skin full."

Tess looked surprised. "Strong constitution I guess?" She sat back down on her bed. "Stronger when I'm not moving though to be fair," she said as she rolled herself back onto her bed.

There was a moment of silence as we both ate croissants.

"Even stronger when I am lying down," came her next comment as she fell backwards onto the bed, dramatically, still munching her croissant.

"In fact, did I hear your mum say she'd brought some tablets?" She went on and almost at once she was back at the

36

tray popping two painkillers out of the foil wrap onto her hand.

"So," she continued as she sat down again on her bed. "I think I remember you being with Josh, or did I dream that?"

I was aware of a huge fat Cheshire cat grin spreading over my face.

"No," I said nodding. "That would be right." I was trying to sound really cool about it but I could feel myself blushing. Why? What is the deal with blushing? Why do I always do that? It makes me feel so stupid and young and hopelessly girly! Which is OK, I guess I am but it doesn't need constant announcing on my cheeks.

Tess sort of clapped her hands together as she snuggled down into bed, I presume hoping calories and painkillers would work their magic.

"Come on then," Tess badgered. "I need to hear all the details."

"Well, not much to tell really. We just chatted—oh and he said he would text me today and maybe we could meet up." I tried to sound sooo casual as I said this, almost mumbling and expected at least a whoop from Tess.

"What? He didn't kiss you?"

People can behave in such unexpected ways. Here I was delighted at a 'meet up' and yet, Tess obviously thought we should have snogged! Why did I now feel a bit disappointed?

"Well, not properly but at one point, he sort of brushed my lips with his." I sighed, it was involuntary, honestly, the sigh that is not the near kiss!

"But let's just get a context here. This is Josh. Generally regarded as Adonis and let's be honest, fancied by you for ages, so in the scheme of things, proper kiss or not, pretty damned exciting."

At this point, she got out of her bed again and started kind of dancing around in an excitable girly way. I couldn't help smiling—that is one of things I do love about Tess, she always seems to do things that I just can't help smiling about.

"I know its BRILLIANT!" I said this kind of kicking my legs in a sort of dead fly dance as I lay on the bed.

"Where will we go this afternoon, not that I mind. I just want to be with him again. Is that really soppy?"

"Well, it's soppy but you are 17, female, and going to see the guy you have fancied for ages—it's probably irrelevant that he is one of the hottest guys in the school, it's your time to be soppy so enjoy it. And you have waited a long time for this. It was before Christmas, wasn't it, when you thought he was going ask you out, then obviously heard what a slapper you really were?"

I threw a pillow at her.

"What on earth do you mean?"

"Joke, babe, just calm down." I had thrown two other pillows and several soft cuddly toys (I know I am 17 what am I doing with lots of cuddly animals—but what do you do with them? They are way too cute to throw out and I haven't got any little brothers or sisters or even cousins or anything. Be honest, they always look forlorn and forgotten in charity shops).

We chatted some more, did a bit of work on a piece of homework (that was brief), went on Facebook to check out comments about the party. Josh had posted himself as 'hopeful', then made this comment about today being an important day for him but it depended on someone else. Way too cryptic for me! Then we showered and Tess left and I set the table as I could smell dinner was well on the way.

Dad was playing something on something—wind instrument I think but not Clarinet, in the lounge. Mum was back from the gym and, having got a good roast on the go, was chatting on the phone. Each time I went into the kitchen, she gesticulated instructions for me—'stir the gravy', 'check the potatoes', that kind of thing. Good job, I am an expert reader of gestures!

Over dinner we chatted about the party. One of the things I don't like about being an only child is that it's all about me. I can't kind of hit the ball to anyone else. I told them I was going out later with Josh—they sort of know about him because, well, we've been at the same school for years and he has been in quite a lot of school shows and stuff.

Of course, I blushed (why why why?) and they noticed and then all this kind of innuendo began about me bringing him home and they even remembered that I said he was one of the hottest (correction, THE hottest) guy in the school. Then they asked me where we were going and I didn't know, and when I'd be back, and I didn't know, so it sounded bit like I was making the whole thing up.

All I knew was the text I had from Josh, just after Tess had left, saying would it be OK to collect me at about 3.30. So of course, not wanting to sound too keen (why do we do this?), I simply replied, fine see you later. I suppose it sounded less desperate than 'anytime is fine, anywhere is fine, as long as it's you coz I've fancied you for ages' which was the alternative.

Chapter 5

It was about 3.35 when my mob rang and he told me he was outside. I had endured simply ages of torture—well, five full minutes since three 3.30. When my brain had circled through thoughts such as, 'What if he doesn't actually turn up?', 'What if I had imagined the way he looked at me at the party and his lips brushing mine?', 'Couldn't have been an accident surely?', 'What if he was doing it for a bet?', 'What if it wasn't really Josh but some alien form inhabiting is body?'.

If it was, would I care, probably not. But anyway, to my great relief, my phone had rung, well played a few bars of Labyrinth.

Important point, he was outside. I yelled cheerio to mum and dad and tried to walk calmly to the front door. I think I have mentioned that our house is kind of long and narrow. Ridiculously long really. I kept feeling that I wanted to break into a jog. Then I struggled to find my coat which somehow had got buried beneath about 50 other coats in the cloakroom.

How can there be that many coats? There are only 3 of us living in the house. God, I sound like my mum when she's moaning about dishes not in the dishwasher. *But he wouldn't just drive off, would he?* I thought to myself as I fought the macs and duffles and kagools of the cloakroom jungle while trying to calm my racing heart.

Then I simply had to check how I looked in the mirror in the hall. I sort of fiddled with my hair, not really achieving anything and put on some lip gloss, then walked in a calm nonchalant and obviously sexy manner to his car. Well, it was his mother's actually but this is an irrelevant detail.

He looked at me and smiled as I got in (have I mentioned how gorgeous he looks when he smiles—OK). I smiled back at him and sighed, hopefully not audibly.

"So the world is our oyster—for a few hours anyway. Where shall we go?"

How come I felt so tongue tied when he was right there listening to me and I so wanted to sound charming and clever and witty.

"I don't know—well, I mean, I don't mind really."

Pathetic with a capital P. I tried to tell myself that actually we got on really well (which we did) and that I had no trouble talking to him last night (which was true and I don't think I was too drunk). I let out a little laugh at myself really but he heard.

"What's so funny then?" He asked.

"Oh nothing, I mean me, I suppose." Oh my God, just listening to myself made me cringe even more. What an incoherent jabbering twit. Thankfully, like the Liesle's suitor in the *Sound of Music* who sings 'you need someone older and wiser telling you what to do' in the song *you are 16 going on 17*—he rescued me, or maybe himself from further incoherent mumblings by coming up with a suggestion.

"Well, as it's not actually raining at the moment, how about we drive over to the Marina and have a walk around the lake there, then a drink at the Abbott Arms. I can't be too late back—bloody course work due in tomorrow."

Talking about school work, now that I could do—for England actually or at least that's what my much cooler mates like Tess would always say when they teased me.

"What? It's due in tomorrow and not done? Shame on you, Josh Crowther."

I could feel I was starting to relax.

"Well, thanks for the support, Miss 'boffin breeches'. It is just about done *actually,* just got to do the references and stuff."

"Watkins said he was going to give us a sociology essay this week as well."

Phew, I thought to myself as the car eased onto the main road from our street something a bit like normal functioning seemed to have returned to my brain.

We chatted about school and lessons and stuff, and it was all OK now. I felt at ease again and like I could chat to him about anything. I even thought I could tell him about Seb but maybe later.

We parked and got out of the car. It was grey and damp. That sort of half-light that we get such a lot of in English winters. But as it was 3.30 so it wouldn't be long till it was proper dark.

"Not warm, is it?" He said as he locked the door. I noticed he glanced at my feet. I was wearing some little boots with my skinny jeans but they probably wouldn't be very waterproof or mud proof.

"We should be OK if we stick to the paths," he said as if reading my mind.

As we started walking, I was wondering whether to get my gloves out of my pocket when he just got hold of my hand.

"Let's go this way," he said as he led the way. "Then we will do most of the loop before we hit the pub and there will only be a short walk back to the car when it's dark."

Honestly, I didn't give a toss. I was with Josh blooming Crowther, that is HOT Josh Crowther and he was HOLDING MY HAND. That must mean he likes me? Right?

For my height, I do have tiny hands, when bored in lessons (yes even the geeky kids like me get bored sometimes—except I'm not really geeky, I just happen to quite like studying but it doesn't mean I hang on to every word that falls from the teachers mouth), I have measured them against the hands of many friends smaller than me and trust me, my hands are little.

But they don't usually *feel* little, but they did now. His hand sort of encompassed mine completely. It felt good.

We chatted about all sorts of stuff as we walked. The universities he'd applied to. Warwick was his top choice but he needed 2 Bs for there, but he explained honestly that he thought that he would get that.

I told him which ones I was looking into and how few did dance courses that didn't major in contemporary and sounded off to him about the relative merits of uni and the stage colleges, no real contest in my mind, performing arts schools would win every time but I still had some convincing to do with dad.

We reached the shingle beach at the far end of the lake and he picked up a stone and sent it skipping over the water—only 2 skips though. I couldn't resist. I chose carefully and threw one, 4 skips, oh yes. There are some advantages to being the only child. I had hours of parental attention, so with patient parents, I had mastered all kinds of surprising skills.

This particular one had been done on a cold beach in Scarborough when we'd been on a brief caravan holiday one year after mum had worried that our regular, at least two a year, holidays abroad did not give me enough of a taste for the traditional English experience, well not of the kind she had as a small child. Dad spent ages with me.

I remember mum telling him off for letting me stay out on the beach for so long as it was freezing. I think my feet went really blue—but I digress.

"Not bad for a girl, eh?" I said tauntingly. So as you can imagine, we spent quite a while launching stones over the water. I was bending forward near the water's edge searching for THE perfect stone to end this battle once and for all when he came up behind me and pushed me forwards, then grabbed me round my waist to stop me from actually stepping into the water.

"Just kidding," he whispered softly into my ear.

I turned around, still in his arms, and he smiled again, then brushed my hair off from my face. He tucked the strand behind my ear and then kissed my cheek. I could feel his warm breath on my ear and my heart pumping in my chest. He kissed my cheek again and then with his hand, he moved my hair from my neck and kissed it, soft light kisses. Well, I am sure by now he could hear my heart pumping, anyone in a mile radius would have been able to hear it.

"I've wanted to do this for a long time," he said as he brought his lips to mine and kissed me lightly, then not so lightly, and it was delicious. His lips were soft and warm, and

I could have stood on that freezing beach for hours with his lips on mine.

"I guess we ought to get to that pub before it's so dark we fall in the lake."

He put his arm around me and we started walking. But every few minutes, we'd sort of look at each other and pause and find ourselves kissing again. It was brilliant. Best cold, damp, dark walk I have had…to date anyway.

The pub was heaving—lots of family groups and celebrations in the restaurant—I guess late lunches. The tables had that 'demolished' look with lots of empty glasses and stains on the white clothes, and people sitting around and chatting while children, a bit bored, wandered off to look at the fish in the indoor fishpond at the entrance.

Balloons that had popped and cocktail swizzlers lay abandoned and forlorn along with empty scrunched up wrapping paper on several of the tables. We headed for the bar which was packed, but just as we walked in, a couple stood up from a little table squashed in the corner and Josh sort of steered me into the seat then went to the bar.

I watched him go to the bar and then watched all the other folk. There were lots of couples and groups of girls and boys, lots of different ages but all unmistakably 'adult'. I sat thinking that it was a bit like another world. The grown-up world I mean, and just then, I felt I was part of it. I was only planning to drink a J2O but that's not the point.

I could see for a moment why Tess was enjoying having a boyfriend and doing couple things and why she wanted me to have one as well—she was right. I could imagine feeling part of this grown-up 'coupled' world. I felt I had been a child forever.

Josh arrived back with the drinks. The table really was quite squashed into the corner, which meant we had to sit really close together—shame! I had taken my coat off while he was at the bar but I had to help him get his off. He nearly knocked a pint out someone's hand (a big bloke who looked like he could have a mean streak to him) when he first tried to pull his arm out of his sleeve.

He took a slurp of his coke, then got hold of my hand.

"Blimey, that's cold," he said as he wrapped my hand in both of his then touched my fingers to his face.

"I'm always like that, sometimes they go really wild sort of colours too, and my feet as well actually. Just the way I am."

"Well, I can't warm your feet up here but give me your other hand, I can certainly get that a bit warmer."

I was deciding if I was going to ask him why he'd given me the cold shoulder treatment before but then also thinking should I risk it when I was having such a lovely time when he stopped rubbing my hand and started fiddling in his coat.

"I've got a present for you. Don't worry, I don't usually go bestowing gifts on every girl I go out with, especially the first time we meet up (*notice he didn't say first date so I was a bit alarmed*), but I have had this for you since Christmas."

He handed me a small square package wrapped in paper with holly leaves all over it. Well wrapped I have to say. My experience is that people generally think women wrap better than blokes, but I have to say in my house, it's a dead giveaway who has wrapped the presents and dad wins hands down.

If mum has wrapped it, you're generally lucky if it doesn't fall out before you get the chance to unwrap it, and guaranteed it will still have the price on.

I held the small package. It was very light—jewellery of some sort I guessed.

Of course, it was almost 6 weeks since Christmas so it all felt a bit odd.

"Well, open it for heaven's sake," he urged.

It was a pair of small, dangly, silver earrings shaped like guitars.

"Oh, they're lovely," I said. "Thank you." I kissed him on the cheek but then he turned his face and we were kissing again—just briefly, of course, we were in a pub and we were grown-ups!

"I have been such a jerk and I am so so sorry," he said. "Mostly for myself cos if I hadn't been such a twit, we might have been going out at Christmas."

"Oh, hold on a minute, what are you on about?"

"Well, it must have been obvious that I fancied you like mad before—remember how we'd chat…" His face clouded over. "Did you not fancy me then, not even a bit?"

"Yes, and I was kind of hoping you would ask me out, but then, well I thought I must have offended you or something because you went from being really friendly to hardly noticing me."

"That's the bit I'm sorry about. I've always thought you were gorgeous, in fact Olivia and I once had a big row because I'd made some comment to that effect (*Oh store this one up to think about/gloat over later I told myself*). But then when we started to chat a bit, it seemed that we really got on well as well."

47

He slurped some more coke. Then he was quiet but patience is not one of my virtues.

"And…" I said with a hint of irritation.

He smiled and put his hand to his head.

"Oh, you are going to think I am such an idiot."

I was fairly sure he was going to say that he'd got drunk at a party and got with someone else and decided I wasn't so gorgeous after all.

"Well, one day—Wednesdays wasn't it we used to wait together—you'd popped to grab a drink from your locker I think and you'd asked me to keep an eye on your bag, and I managed to knock it over." He paused.

"What?" I jumped in. "And you thought I would think 'clumsy guy serial bag destroyer? Don't get involved'."

He was smiling.

"No, course not, but when your bag tipped over, something fell out. A pregnancy testing kit."

I was mid-swallow with a mouthful of apple mango J2O which I nearly spat out at him as I started to laugh.

I gained control of my upper digestive tract. But then as my brain raced, I saw another side to things, not so light-hearted.

"So, let me get this straight, because you thought I may have needed a pregnancy testing kit, you thought 'oh no! Slut or slapper, leave well alone, Joshie boy; step away from the girl with dubious morals'."

"No! No, it wasn't like that at all. I really felt for you. I was awake all that night thinking I could still go out with you and be this really supportive boyfriend, but then I thought maybe you would just always see me as more of a mate and we do get on well, but I was not thinking of you as a mate. So after tossing and turning for a long time, thinking of all different scenarios, I thought actually the most caring thing to do would be to do nothing.

"No extra pressure for you, not put you in any kind of difficult position—well other than possibly being pregnant. So I thought I would just carry on being 'matey' but I couldn't really. I had really got used to the idea that with a bit of luck, you would be my girlfriend."

He took another mouthful of coke and smiled as he continued, "Thing is our family always have this big social do on boxing day and I had planned that we'd be going out by then and I would invite you round and give you your Christmas present then. I can see now that I should probably have just talked to you about it all, but come on, it's quite a tough call. But I never mentioned it to anyone and I figured that I'd hear on the old school jungle telegraph if you were."

He paused briefly and I jumped in again, my brain whirling.

"So let me just get this straight now. You wanted to go out with me but just as you planned to ask me out, you thought I might be pregnant so you gave me a wide berth (sorry unintentional semantic pun) and expect me to believe you just kept it to yourself and cried over your Christmas crackers?"

"Well, let me just get this straight. Are you thinking I shouldn't have been upset over you or that I should have asked you out anyway, which I wanted to do but I…well, I think cared too much to do that."

"So it wouldn't bother you if I was pregnant now?"

He did look surprised.

"Are you? You don't look it and I thought by now you would and when I saw you knocking back cider, or correct me, was it vodka the other night, I convinced myself you couldn't possibly be pregnant. You would be far too responsible to drink if you were."

"But not too responsible to avoid getting pregnant in the first place?"

"Hey, hold on, I'm not really trying to judge you. I just wanted to explain why I had been such a nutcase and not asked you out sooner. I know I was a jerk. I'm not proud of how I acted, though I could have been worse, you know talked to other folks and stuff."

He smiled and I melted and he moved closer and kissed me, and that was good because it must have been at least ten minutes since the last kiss and I had forgotten how good it was.

I decided it was my turn to be honest now.

"You are a jerk really."

He put on a hurt look which made me melt again.

"I never was pregnant. I never even had the teeniest tiniest worry that I might be *(It didn't seem either the right time or completely cool to 'fess up' to the fact that I was definitely still a virgin)*. It was a prop for my musical theatre exam. I thought I had told you that I was reciting a monologue from *Dear Nobody*."

He looked lost.

"It's a book and in it, the girl does get pregnant and talks in her head to the baby."

"So it was just a prop?"

I nodded. "It was just a prop." I had this uncontrollable urge to giggle so bit my lip.

"Just a prop."

My lip biting didn't work and I sniggered, then he smiled and I creased up, and he started to laugh too. Phew.

"Did we just nearly have our first row over a prop?"

I couldn't answer, I was concentrating on not peeing myself. But he was right so I nodded.

When we went outside, it was completely dark and drizzling. We walked back towards the car getting dripped on by the trees. We reached the car and he put his arm round my waist. My coat was loose and his hands were inside my jacket as he pulled me towards him. We kissed and he pulled me really close. I could feel his whole body pressed against me and I just wanted that moment to go on forever.

When I was little, mum and I used to talk about bottle moments—you know those moments that feel so good, you just want to remember every detail so that you can keep them forever and whenever you need to. If you are down or sad about something, you can get the bottle off some fictitious shelf in your brain and just enjoy a bit of it again. Well, this was one of those. Oh yes!

I don't know how long we stood there, but take it from me, it wasn't long enough. We'd sort of stop and just peck each other on the lips and then somehow start all over again. Eventually, he hugged me to him and buried his face in my neck. I noticed my hair felt damp and cold so we must have stood in the rain kissing for some time.

"Don't laugh," he said, "but I really have been just waiting for this for so long. I think I'm just not going to be able to wipe the smile off my face for weeks."

I smiled and my hands were round his neck so I sort of ran my fingers through his hair where it curled over his collar.

"I just don't want to let you go, I'm scared something will happen."

"Don't be so daft, you muppet!" was my compassionate loving reply. "Just think about sociology tomorrow so you will see me then."

"Oh God, yeah and coursework for me tonight. I guess I ought to get you home."

"I've got a late start on Mondays which is pretty cool, isn't it, so a lie in for me tomorrow and then sociology at 11."

"If you come in at 10.45, then I could have a hot chocolate waiting for you and you'd get to see me at break."

"Sounds like a plan," I said calmly.

He kissed me again and pulled me even closer. It was just brill brill brill!

Then he took me home. What's that saying about all good things ending, well it's true and it sucks!

Chapter 6

As I walked through the hall, I heard the unmistakable 'be doop be doo' of the renowned phone in CTU, so I knew dad was engrossed in his catch up game with the episodes of 24 he'd recorded—I think he's at least a series behind. As a wise daughter, I chose not to disturb him. I also knew mum would not be in the lounge as she hates it.

I walked through to the breakfast room and sure enough, mum was sitting there in the cosy fluffy pink, in the 'Per Una' dressing gown I had bought her last Christmas. She had a load of papers spread out on the table and a glass of red wine in her hand.

"Well, someone looks like they had a good time."

I guess I was still grinning from ear to ear like a lemon. I nodded and sat down at the table opposite her.

"Come on, you've got to give me more than a nod!"

"Yeah, it was good, we got on really well."

"So will you be seeing him again?"

"Yes, tomorrow in sociology as it happens." Two can tease, I thought, as she rolled her eyes at me.

"Hey, don't try and be tooo cool. I mean at 17 if you go out with a guy and you don't come back grinning like a

Cheshire cat, then there is something wrong. I mean you certainly shouldn't bother a second time."

Ouch, I thought. I must try to be cooler at school if my own mother thought I was grinning like a Cheshire cat. I needed to go for a distant, not very interested in anything look.

"Have I ever told you about Davy Bridgeson?" I shook my head, as all teenagers know there are sometimes when you just have to allow parents to tell you things. You may have heard it before or not, you may be interested or not, but you just have to go with it. I sensed this was one of those moments.

"I was about your age and I had fancied him for ages. He was tall, but broadish as well, and had dark curly hair and a moustache, which I thought was very grown-up. My father had a moustache, do you think there was deep dark psychological reason why I fancied him?"

(*She paused but so briefly that she clearly hadn't wanted me to comment—I made an 'I haven't a clue but please let's not discuss it' face and shrugged my shoulders and she continued.*)

"Anyway, we went to the same youth group, attached to a church, but we were sort of in different groups. So he was always with this particular crowd, and though I knew them all, I just wasn't part of the group. There were some really pretty girls I might add in his crowd.

"One I remember particularly, Claire; she was called and she was really petite but sort of curvy and she had this long really ringlet curled hair. Never spoke to her much but kind of hated her from a distance because I just knew he simply must fancy her."

Mum stopped to take a sip or two from her glass and then refilled it from the bottle on the table. I knew she was just having a breather and the tale would go on. And I was right.

"So one night, we'd been at this social. He'd been playing pool with his crowd and I'd been chatting and stuff with my mates. I had chatted to him a couple of times before—well, I say chatted. I always seemed to lose the power of coherent speech when he talked to me but I'd stuttered through a few conversations *(So that's where the incoherent stuttering gene comes from I thought).*

"Then this night, we just seemed to catch each other's eye a lot and smile at each other. I suppose I hoped he'd come over and chat. But no! And then it got to when it was time to go and my mate, Pat, said I should go and talk to him, but you know how it is. He was with all his mates and I just couldn't walk over to him in the middle of a game of pool and start chatting. So I sidled off with my mates and went home."

She paused again and had another slurp.

"It was Sunday night and I went home and had a bath. I had just got dried and put on my dressing gown, hair wet and in a towel, when the doorbell goes. Well, I never expected it would be for me, then dad's shouting upstairs. I go down and there he is Davy at my door. Talk about gobsmacked and horrified all at the same time.

"No makeup, towel round my hair and dressing gown, thick, turquoise and candlewick, not sort of black and silky and sexy. Anyway, he said his mates said he must deliver this and he handed me a letter in an envelope. Then he said to me 'please say yes' and just turned and went. My dad made lots of dodgy comments about boys calling round late at night and me in my dressing gown.

"Dad asked what he'd been wanting and I said my watch had fallen off and he'd returned it. By this time, I had shoved the letter in my pocket. So I went to my room and read it and to this day, it has got to be the second most romantic letter I have ever received in my life."

I jumped. "What, really just the second?"

"Well yes, but only coz he wrote me another one, but don't be jumping the gun. The letter was all about how he'd fancied me for ages and tried to get to talk to me but we both always seemed to be surrounded but other people. All his mates knew he fancied me because apparently, he couldn't stop talking about me, so they'd eventually said he simply had to ask me out because he was just getting boring."

"So did you go out with him?"

"Yes, first time we went for this walk in sort of woods and it was lovely, so romantic and we held hands and he kissed me, and it was all just brilliant. And after that first date, he wrote this other really slushy romantic letter—still got it in the loft in with all my 'precious' bits and pieces. I mean he wasn't my first boyfriend but he was really special; he really seemed to make my heart pound."

"So if it was sooo good, what happened?"

"Well, we went out for ages, about 2 years I think, maybe a bit less. He'd left school and worked for the civil service. I think he was probably about three years older than me. It was great because he could drive. When I was doing A levels, he'd pick me up some nights from school and I always felt kind of grown-up.

"He wanted us to get engaged but I couldn't. I knew I wanted to go to university and I knew that if I got engaged to him that would be it and I would never leave Hartington. It just sort of fell apart after that because we both knew it wasn't going anywhere. But…" Mum sighed.

"….it was brilliant while it lasted. He was probably what I'd call my first love and that is…well, it's special, whatever happens later."

Mum refilled her glass again and offered me some. I have to say that red wine is one of my least favourite alcoholic drinks but just like listening to the story, I felt saying yes was the right thing to do as she was obviously trying to treat me like a grown-up. I sipped and decided again that it would take serious dedication to get to like wine!

"So what about your evening?"

"It was good I already said—oh I must tell you one thing though. Remember when I did my Trinity exam?"

Mum nodded.

"And remember how I mentioned Josh then and said we used to chat coz he played guitar and I remember asking dad something about tuning different strings for him?"

"Yes, I wondered then if he was going to be the new guy on the scene but then he seemed to disappear."

"Well, two things. First, he bought me a Christmas present." I fished the earrings out of my coat pocket.

"Not great on time keeping then?"

I ignored the remark.

"Look, aren't they lovely?"

"Oh, they are! So, good taste but crap time keeping!"

I started to giggle a bit.

"Well, apparently, he knocked my bag over one time and the pregnancy testing kit fell out and he said he backed off because he thought if I was pregnant then he didn't want to add any other pressure."

Mum started to laugh as well.

"Oh honestly, didn't we joke about how rumours could start with that as a prop."

We both giggled for a moment and I remember thinking how nice it was drinking wine giggling with mum about NOT being pregnant.

"So I guess you could take another view and say he was a heel because he could have been honest about it and maybe he actually thought you were 'easy', 'a slut', I don't know what the terminology is these days, and he was better off to leave well alone."

"I said the same thing to him—but he does seem really nice—I suppose he convinced me that wasn't the reason."

"Did he ask you then or had he found out that you weren't?"

"Well, he said he'd guessed I couldn't have been or else he'd have heard. And he's right there, you can't keep that sort of secret in a school, someone always seems to let slip."

"Well, that sounds true, nothing ever seems so gossip worthy as other people's misfortune!"

Mum took another sip and I noticed both of our glasses were getting emptied.

"Is that how you would see it then?" I asked her. "If I was pregnant, would you think oh that's unfortunate?"

"Oh my God, are you?"

I shook my head laughing again and nearly spurting out wine.

"Well, yes, in lots of ways I would. I mean I think it's unnecessary these days. It's funny that sex seems to be sung about and talked about and is in every magazine, yet still girls seem to get pregnant when they don't want to…and while we are on the subject…"

I held up my hand and shook my head still laughing.

"No, NO, not the pep talk again please!"

"Sometimes in life things happen that we don't intend or at a time we don't intend but a lot worse things in life can happen than having a baby that's for sure. But don't get me wrong, I don't think its plan A and you'd have a lot of hard decisions to make. And it would be tough to go to uni and…"

I stopped her.

"Look, I'm not, it was just interesting the way you said it. Like it wouldn't be the end of the world."

WE both fell silent and then dad walked in and somehow we both started laughing like silly school girls. I suppose it was the wine it seems to make folk conspiratorial and giggly!

"What did I do that was so funny?" He asked as he walked past.

"Oh nothing, honey," said mum. "Just girl talk."

Dad noticed the empty bottle and picked it up.

"Wine talk more like it," he said in a silly slurred kind of voice.

I decided it was probably time to head to bed. I had felt my phone vibrating in my pocket and guessed it would be Tess wanting all the 'gories'.

"Are you off up, love? It's still early, don't you want some food?" Mum asked and I nodded.

"Yes to bed but no to food—I fancy a bath and then I might watch something on catch up."

"It's your late start tomorrow, isn't it? But dad and I will be off very early to get the train to London—it's that conference I mentioned and dad has to see someone about

…something musical I forget what but we won't be back till quite late either."

"That's fine—remember I'm 17 now and quite able to look after myself," I said this in a very supercilious and silly voice.

"Hmmmmmm," was mum's response.

But then she called, "Night, love," as I walked into the hall.

As soon as I was in room, I looked at my phone—6 missed calls, all Tess, and 4 new messages, 2 from Tess and 2 from Josh. Needless to say, I read and replied to the Josh ones first then got ready for bed and rang Tess once I was comfortable in bed. I knew it would be a long convo.

I was shattered. I remember telling Tess all about Josh and I remember thinking if I was listening to myself talking about him, I would think 'Oh my God how sickly and gooey and pukey…' but it didn't feel like that all. I don't really remember falling asleep but I felt all warm and glowy again.

Chapter 7

I woke when it was still dark. I guess I had heard the front door close as mum and dad left for the station—it's impossible to close the door without a struggle which always means it's noisy. But it could have been the rain which was torrential and seemed to be angled with all its force onto the window right by my bed. I glanced at my phone for the time, it was only 6.30.

I worked out in my mind that as I didn't need to be at school till 10, which meant leaving at 9.30, I could go back to sleep for at least another 2 hours. I snuggled down under my quilt again but realised I was actually wide awake. I guess I had slept really soundly. I lay for a few minutes reliving some of the best Josh moments, then somehow almost without thinking, I was out of bed still in dressing gown and pulling on some wellies in the cloakroom.

As soon as I walked out of the back door, I could see the door of the play house was ajar, ever so slightly, and knew he was there or had just left. My first thought was right. He had the blanket I had left draped around his shoulders and he looked utterly miserable—couldn't blame him, the air was really damp and cold.

I didn't go right in, I just asked him out straight. And it wasn't planned, not consciously; it's like I was acting on some sort of auto-pilot. I didn't ever actually remember thinking 'mum and dad are out and I don't need to be at school till late so Seb can come and have a decent breakfast' but that was pretty much what came out of my mouth.

He didn't answer but stood up so I went ahead and he followed me into the kitchen. I did a quick check on the cupboard and fridge and found beans, sausages, eggs and bread, and he nodded when I suggested that as a menu. While the sausages were frying, I made 2 steaming mugs of hot chocolate and he sat down at the breakfast bar hands around his cup while I busied about in my dressing gown being Miss Domesticated, cooking the breakfast.

He remained pretty silent and I thought that as he would probably prefer a breakfast that wasn't too burnt, I should wait until the food was safely on the plate before I engaged him conversation. I confess to scepticism about this whole idea that people can multitask, quite simply I am challenged in the multitasking department!

He seemed contented enough though, sipping his drink and looking at things in the kitchen. We had a big notice board by the breakfast bar and on it were letters from school, invites to parties, dance school info, course work due dates, plumbers numbers, the usual family stuff, but I noticed him at one point reading them intently. He also seemed to study, systematically, the paintings that were on the opposite wall.

All done by me, mostly very childish, but I guess evidence of parents who cared deeply and praised and valued all my achievements, however small judging by the stick man drawings, by giving them a frame and a place on the wall of the kitchen. I almost felt ashamed of this.

I wasn't sure if it was because I felt guilty because it was something he didn't have or because I felt too old to still have such things on the wall, and maybe he would think I was mollycoddled or babied in some way. Maybe I was.

I piled two plates up with food and sat down at the breakfast bar with him. He looked at mine and asked, "Is that all you're having?"

"Actually," I replied. "Sausage, bacon, an egg, toast, and beans is quite a big breakfast for me."

"Yeah, but you've given me more!"

"Sorry, just leave it if it's too much; it's just most of the boys I know seem to eat like elephants."

"I'll see what I can do," he said and he smiled as he attacked the plate of food. I was struck by how young he looked when he smiled.

"Well, looks like you did OK," I said when he stuffed the last piece of toast into his mouth.

He nodded still chewing.

He shook his head.

"Do all girls feel like they have to talk all the time or is it just the ones I seem to come across?"

"Hey, I hardly said a word while you ate—or while I was cooking actually!"

He smiled again, and again, I thought how young his face seemed.

"So did you get to see your sister?" His smile vanished like he had just turned it off with some switch.

He nodded. "Her! Yes! God, she is such a fucking twat, she just messes everything up all the time."

"What on earth has she done?"

"Been stupid! Been a twat! Again!"

I didn't answer. If I'm honest, I didn't really know what to say, so I went to the fridge and got some fresh orange juice and two glasses. I poured the juice and sat down again. He downed the whole glass in one, then said, "Got herself knocked up! Stupid twat!"

"Well, it wasn't all her fault," I said with some sort of female defensive thing going on.

He shook his head and I noticed that when he did that, he looked like some old care worn weary bloke, which seemed such a contrast to how he looked when he smiled.

"Deeerrrrhhh," was his response, which made me feel that maybe it was a silly childish comment.

"So has she decided what she's going to do?"

"Way too late for that now, so yes, I suppose she has. I did know she was pregnant before but when I saw her, she was huge and it…well it's just stupid she's just ruined everything…again."

I was just wondering what to say next when he shook his head again and said, "You see, she always messes things up. We had this plan for me and her that when she was 16, she'd get a flat or a hostel place near wherever I was and then I could go and stay with her sometimes. We could even go and see dad, mind you she was never as keen as me on that idea!

"Then when I was 16, we'd get a place together and be sort of normal I suppose. We'd talked about getting a job as well and stuff like having mates round you know but she's gone and ruined all that now."

"Well, you could still do that. Unless she's going to live with her boyfriend I suppose."

He made a face that implied this wasn't likely.

"Thing is, she was going to finish with him anyway. Well, she said she tried to but he got a bit, you know, macho. Gave her a bit of a battering so she didn't want him to know that she was going to have a baby."

"Well, it sounds like she's well out of it."

"Yeah, but she also says he found out somehow and is looking for her."

"But she'll be safe if she's still in the care home, won't she?"

"Yeah, but she sort of wanders, a bit like me. If things upset her, she takes off and I told her she mustn't coz that's when he might find her."

"Where does she know him from anyway—he sounds like a right waster, or worse!"

I knew he was pretty free with swearing but somehow, as the older person, it didn't feel right, so I didn't say the word I might have that rhymes with banker.

"You can say that again. He's older. But we both met him in one of the first care homes we went to. He's left care now. He's into drugs. At one point, she thought he probably sold them as well. She ran into him one night when she was out of the home—when she shouldn't been. Then she took to leaving whenever she wanted to see him."

"Don't they stop her, at the home I mean. Surely it's not safe."

"They aren't allowed to, really its sort of imprisonment if you lock doors or rooms and stuff, and to be honest, if you really want to go, it's quite easy. I mean you can just walk out and they can't stop you. They will 'restrain' you…" He used his fingers to add quotation marks "…if you are going to hurt someone else but if you just walk out calmly, I don't think they are allowed to restrain you unless they have actual evidence that you are going to do something to harm yourself…or maybe someone else."

"So do you just walk back when you have had enough or need a meal or whatever."

"Sometimes! Other times, police might spot you coz they have to let the police know that you've left. Other times, you can let the police pick you up."

"What by being somewhere you know they'll be looking?"

He sort of laughed.

"Yeah, I guess or taking something from a shop and forgetting to pay but making it obvious, shop picking, then they call the police, you go to the station, they run a check and you get taken back. If you end up a long way away, that's easier on the legs."

"And don't the police get sick of you doing it? I mean it seems a nightly kind of thing with you, oh and it's shop lifting, not picking." I know, it's true I sound like some governess from a bygone era. He gave me a pointed look which told me he would ignore that particular comment.

"Well, that's why I don't involve police all the time—if they get sick of you, they can make it…sort of not very nice— keep you waiting for ages or be a bit rough when they cuff you."

"I hate the police," I said, maybe I was searching for some sort of solidarity some point of agreement in two very different lives. Maybe I was at that moment wanting to sound cool! Pathetic, absolutely pathetic.

He laughed.

"You! How can you hate the police? I don't suppose you've had any contact and I'm pretty sure you will never have spent a night in the cells?"

I almost felt myself blushing. I felt pretty stupid but carried on anyway.

"You're right but I have got 2 'police stories'—both showing how rotten they can be."

"Well," he said, like he was being patient with a wayward child about to confess something or make some unnecessarily elaborate excuse.

"OK! First, I was quite little, it wasn't long after we moved into this house. I was probably about 6 and one day, I came home with mum in the car and the road was all blocked off. Police at each end and they wouldn't even let residents up the streets or tell us what was going on, so we went to a mate's and didn't get back into the house till about midnight. It turns out that some chap had got drunk, locked himself out of his house and tried to break in.

"Someone saw him and reported him to the police thinking he was a burglar. But then he was waving this toy gun—sorry 'imitation firearm'—at the police and basically after a 'siege situation', they shot him and he died. He was only about 30 I think. I mean surely they could have seen it wasn't a real gun—he obviously didn't fire it and if they were going to shoot him, surely they could have aimed at his leg or arm or something?"

He nodded and then raised his eyebrows as if telling me to continue.

"Well, now to the second. It was a Saturday night and I and mum and dad had just got a Chinese takeaway and we were going to watch a DVD so were all in the lounge. Well, this house is long and thin, and if you are in the front of the house, you often won't hear what's going on in the kitchen.

"But suddenly, there was this really loud knocking at the front door and when dad opened the lounge door, there was this policeman stood there, already inside the house like he'd come in from the back. And another one at the front door. It was all a sort of shock but they started saying how our security wasn't good and they had noticed some bikes in the back that weren't locked away and said we needed better locks on the back door.

"It was ridiculous but it all happened so fast, they sort of frog marched dad though the house to the back and were banging on about locks and stuff, and then they left. And it was then when mum and dad and I talked about it, over cold Chinese food I may add, that we realised neither of them had numbers on their epaulettes and it was weird the way they had come into the house.

"Anyway next day, the bikes had all been stolen from the shed and when we, well dad, spoke to the police, they said police would never enter a house without either a warrant or permission so they were bogus cops I guess."

"Hardly seems fair to hold that against the real cops though," he replied.

"I know it's just the two experiences I have had don't seem positive."

"I thought most people like you would look up to the cops as they help keep riff raff at bay, keep the streets safe."

"Well, I hardly think they do that! I can't count how many times our sheds have been broken into and bikes or other stuff stolen and the police always seem to suggest it's our fault in some way—once we'd padlocked all three bikes to the big pear tree in the garden but someone cut through the chain with bolt cutters and the police said we should have put them in the shed.

"When we explained we'd had them stolen from there too, he said maybe we should keep them in the house. That hardly seems an answer, does it?"

"Yeah, I can see it was disconcerting," he said as he nodded.

"It's disconcerting actually, there isn't a word disconcerting…" Honestly the words were out of my mouth before I realised what I was doing; my inner governess self was determined to surface. He shot me a daggered look.

"…though disconcerting would make much more sense," I conceded because honestly it would!

"Well, you've got to be careful, haven't you? All these unsavoury types hanging about there and they might see a nice shed and think 'that looks like an OK place to hide out for a bit'."

He smiled again at his own joke. I think and I smiled too, then I noticed the time on the clock on the wall and panicked.

"Oh my God! Is that the time. Sorry look, I've got to get ready for school."

I quickly put stuff into the dishwasher and he stood up and was heading for the door. Just before he opened it, I said, "I wish I could talk to my mum about you and your sister. I'm sure she'd be able to think of some way of helping."

He shook his head. "Nah, trust me, social workers are awful, not being rotten about your mum, but they are—worse than police, in my book. At least I know where I am with the cops and they don't try and pretend that really they are my mates."

And then he was out of the door before I could say anything else. When I went upstairs to shower and get ready, I noticed I'd had several missed calls and texts. I decided I'd read them on my way to school."

Chapter 8

When I checked the messages, four were from Josh. The first two were lovely, saying how he couldn't wait to see me and was almost counting the minutes. The second two were more 'why aren't you answering your phone' type messages. There were also some missed calls from Tess and a message from mum. I sent a quick reply to mum then went as fast as I could to school calculating that I should just about make it before sociology started.

I could hear the bell going as I walked into the school grounds but decided to head straight for the sixth form common room. The door opened and people started filing out just as I neared, so I stopped. Within seconds, Josh appeared. At first I wondered if he was going to be frosty but his face just lit up into one of those heart melting smiles as soon as he saw me. He came over and said 'Hi'.

"Thought maybe you had decided not to bother with school today?"

I laughed. "No, it's just, well I got up then went downstairs and then…fell asleep on the sofa and my phone was still upstairs."

I had one of those cockerel crowing moments like Judas when he betrayed Jesus. I know this is different scale altogether, but here I was lying to my brand new boyfriend, who I had wanted to go out with for ages and who, I hoped, I would want to go out with me for ages, and who I hoped would never lie to me about why he wasn't answering my calls.

The thing is, I did want to tell him, honestly. I wanted to ask him what I should do. I felt, especially now Seb had told me about his sister and her being pregnant, that I ought to tell someone but I didn't want Seb to think I was just another busy body.

I really did want to chat to Josh about it but we'd started walking to the social sciences block and were nearing the door, already a long way behind everyone else so it just didn't seem like the kind of thing you could drop into a conversation without some explanation. 'Oh sorry I couldn't get you call as I was entertaining a young homeless lad for breakfast, as you do!'

"Well, not to worry, you woke up in time and you're here and…"

I was just about to push open the door to the block when he grabbed my arm and kind of pulled me round the side of the building and kissed me for what felt like a lovely long time.

"I've been waiting since yesterday to do that again," he said. "…and I want to do it again already but we don't want the wrath of Heaton on our heads, do we?"

I laughed and we raced into the block and to the classroom. Luckily, textbooks were still being given out, etc., so we muttered 'sorries' and got into our seats.

"Right," said Mr Heaton as we were sitting down. "Today, we are beginning the module on homelessness. Let's begin with a few statistics, but first any ideas on which groups of people are most likely to become homeless?"

"People just out of prison."

"Yes, that's right, Aaron." Mr Heaton started writing on the board and different folks chipped in.

"Nutters…ow," Paul said and had then been promptly thumped by Kirsty sitting next to him.

"People with no family."

"Kids who've been in care."

"Addicts."

"Ex-servicemen."

"What about women? I haven't seen many women on the streets," Jasminder asked.

"Good question, and yes, there are women who are homeless but statistically less women than men." Mr Heaton paused for a moment after he'd answered her question.

"Well, that covers most of the main categories," he went on, as he checked what he'd written on the smart board. "But we need to think a bit more about what we mean by homelessness. How accurate do you think the statistics are?"

"Well, I don't suppose they survey all the 'Big Issue' sellers? But maybe they do?" Ellis commented.

"Also some people may be don't have a home but stay with mates!"

"I know sofa surfing like Sheeran," said Fahim.

"Or squat!"

"Or die!" This was Paul again.

"Lots of good thoughts and as you brought the subject up, any guesses as to what the life expectancy of someone who is homeless would be?"

Various people shouted out numbers but Mr Heaton just wrote 42 in big letters on the board.

We then had to split into groups to do some worksheets which was pretty interesting really. It was lovely working with Josh (and others). We did work but he would keep kind of catching my eye and smiling and if I hadn't found the topic so interesting I'd have been having all sorts of other thoughts.

Eventually, sir brought the class back together for a summary which he wrote on the board—some statistics and the problems in gathering any kind of 'meaningful' (important word in any essay we write which mentions statistics) data, reasons for homelessness, and the homework we had to do.

We were just starting to kind of gather things when Paul chirped up again.

"So in summary, Sir, we could say that the homeless represent all the inadequates we have in our society? Mentally ill, addicts, learning disabled, social misfits asylum seekers and delinquents?"

"Well, certainly, the vulnerable groups in society are perhaps most at risk but it's an inappropriate value judgement to label them the way you just did, Paul…" Mr Heaton was going to go on but Paul interrupted.

"Oh, I know vulnerable and needy but you know survival of the fittest and frankly, they're the ones who can't make it so maybe we should just stop them being a drain on the rest of us?"

I could tell lots of folks were getting annoyed and wanting to say something but also it was right near the end of the lesson and no wanted to delay getting to lunch.

"Well, Paul, there are lots of very valued members of society who need a bit of support and millions of people need a bit of support for a time, like when you broke your leg skiing last year but we didn't just write you off, did we? We sent homework and moved some classes so when you came back on crutches, you didn't have to go upstairs."

"Yeah, but you knew I would be all right again. Some of these…I don't know…these young delinquents, what hope have they really got. OK, they've been in care and that's tough but what are they really going do? Drink, smoke, get into drugs then crime, have babies they can't look after, and probably end up in prison!"

I remember kind of phasing out and just thinking *Oh my God, they're talking about Seb*. It was like somehow it wasn't just a statistic, it was real people. I didn't even really feel like I was going to cry but I just felt tears streaming down my face.

"Sadly, that's true but surely, as a society, we have a duty to try and help?" Mr Heaton was continuing but I was just willing the lesson to end but also wishing I could come up with a really good argument to just shut Paul up. I thought of loads later.

"Well, that is the humanitarian or sentimental approach but surely we have to count the cost. Not just financially but in human terms—I mean there will be another generation of messed up kids to just keep the whole thing going and they are just one part of the 'homeless problem'."

The class were getting quite restless now and people had started shouting out things like 'fascist' and 'Nazi'.

Mr Heaton broke in. "Well, let's all just take a breath. I am sure that Paul was probably just being devil's advocate to get us all thinking and he has raised some points. It will be useful to discuss next time but for now, lunch, and remember the homework."

Everyone started to leave but I didn't want to stand up as tears were literally streaming now and I was wanting to sob and howl in quite a ridiculous fashion.

Josh twigged I was crying. Well, if I'm honest, it was blatantly obvious, and he put his arm around me and kind of shepherded me out of class and into the quad, and then we walked away from the general crowds that were milling around going for lunch and headed towards the gate. Josh was brill; he just kept his arm round me and sort of kept me walking and he didn't even ask what the matter was.

He even helped me fish a tissue out of my pocket and he was carrying my coat, which he must have grabbed from the classroom. We walked out of the main gates and up the lane. There was a bench about half way up the lane and we sat down. I think I had stopped sobbing by then but my nose was running still and I was breathing in that kind of gulpy way you do when you've just stopped having a good bawl.

"Look, I don't want you to think I'm in the habit of luring young ladies away from school but whatever this is all about, I'm not sure you're in the right frame of mind for school this afternoon, so how about I walk you home?"

I nodded my response, my head was forward and I was trying to hide my face with my hair. He bent round in front of me and put his hand under my chin and lifted it slowly and just gently kissed me. I didn't really want him to just then but somehow it would have taken more emotional energy to stop it than to just enjoy it, which I did.

"God, I must look awful!" I said when our lips separated.

"Well, I'm not wild about the black cheeks but it's still you and I think you're gorgeous."

"Thanks, I mean thanks for just being so nice and not badgering me with questions."

"Well, I don't like seeing you upset so I suppose I would like to know what it's all about but let's get you home and you can get freshened up. You might feel more like talking then?" He stroked my head as he spoke and I could feel I was welling up again.

"Don't be too nice to me though," I said smiling but crying all at the same time.

Josh laughed.

"Come on, let's get you home," he said as he stood up and held my coat for me.

We walked home holding hands and he would occasionally make a funny remark about someone we passed or something about school, I think to try and make me laugh, which generally it did, but every time I laughed, I seemed to end up in tears again.

I let us into the house and he said should he go but I said it would be really nice if he stayed. I went upstairs and tried to sort out my face but it was obvious pretty quickly that time was needed to sort out the puffy eyes and red nose, but at least I got rid of the mascara all down my cheeks.

We headed into the kitchen and I was just giving him options on juices we had in the fridge when I suddenly heard myself saying, "Look, not wanting you to think I'm the kind of girl that regularly gets guys to take her home then plies them with drink, but I really do fancy something stronger than juice and there's this bottle of cold white wine, what do you reckon?"

"Well, wine is not my usual choice but it sounds fine to me, and just for the record, please feel free to lead me astray in any way you want!"

It wasn't 'my' drink either but I did really feel like having some alcohol. So, we sort of settled ourselves on the sofa in the lounge with the wine and a few crisps and sandwiches, and flicked on the TV. I was feeling a lot more settled now and I did want to tell him about Seb but thought I'd wait till he asked what had been the matter which I was sure he would.

"I must confess," I said swallowing the last of a Tuna sandwich, "that this is the first time I've missed school when I've not been really ill; first time I've brought a guy back to the house in the middle of the day and drunk wine. But it feels good. I guess I've been missing out."

I was feeling much calmer now and Josh and I were just enjoying chatting. He mentioned that tomorrow night there was some sort of supper thing that Tess and Jack were going to and would I like to go too. At first, I said I wasn't sure that I hadn't been invited but he said it was Jack's folks that were having the 'do' and I knew from Tess that Josh and Jack had been great mates from when they were young kids.

So I said yes, of course. I also thought Tess wouldn't forgive me for passing up on such a chance. We kept kissing and chatting then and I don't know why but I asked him about Olivia and particularly about why they had broken up. He seemed to be very honest. They'd got on well but after a while, he said it just felt like a habit and they both felt they needed a break—and he said he had begun to 'notice' other girls like me.

I know what you'll be thinking reading this—that he was just flattering me and yes he probably was. But you know, I could live with that. He asked me about Alex who I'd gone out with in year 11. Alex had been very into football, and very good, and was on the same team as Josh for a while. I could even confess, not that I am proud of it you understand, to watching Josh on occasions when I was there supporting Alex.

I suppose I sort of realised then that Alex and Josh were kind of mates they would have no doubt been on football tours, etc. together even though at school they were in different years. Then he just came right out and asked if I'd slept with Alex. I suppose I felt a bit affronted, but I don't know why, so I turned it straight back on him. He answered by just sort of explaining that he'd gone out with Olivia for ages, the assumption being that obviously they had.

But then added, smiling, that they were very careful (quite what that means I'm not sure!) and that she had certainly never had occasion to need a pregnancy testing kit. I still hadn't actually answered his question. I think part of me didn't want him to know that I was still a virgin. I mean I wasn't nun like with Alex but we had stopped short of actual sex of the 'could get you pregnant' kind.

My mind was racing a bit with thoughts of whether he would think me young and stupid or sort of frigid, so I was wanting to change the subject when he went on that after he'd seen the kit and thought I was pregnant, he thought to himself that if the rumours came about that Alex had been the dad, he'd have made sure Alex did the right thing.

I couldn't decide then whether he was just showing a really nice, caring side to his character or was he sussing out whether I would sleep with him. Which would be okay, he was 18, I was 17, hardly children. I had thought to myself after

Alex and I had finished that the next guy would be the one I'd sleep with and I was even on the pill coz mum had sort of insisted that 'you never know when you may decide to'. I think she was secretly worried about drunken parties when caution and better judgement are thrown to the wind, but really I'm not like that.

I'm the sensible one who will stop before I'm legless and often I'm the one who makes sure my mates get home. I remember more than one occasion when I have argued with mates trying to tell them that they'll regret something, varying from dancing on a table to snogging the guy they never liked—but of course they never listen at the time and have nothing but vague memories (if any) and self-recriminations afterwards.

I had certainly determined to myself that when I did decide to go all the way with someone for the first time, I certainly didn't want to be drunk.

Josh and I were still sat on the sofa with reruns of Friends on the TV. We were kissing again and his hands were kind of wandering over me as we kissed and it was wonderful. Then Josh suddenly pulled away.

"What was that?" He asked.

"What?"

"That noise sounded like a door banging."

"Oh, it probably was—shouldn't worry, our old windows are so draughty that gales blow through them even when they are shut." I was very reassuring because I did really want to get back to kissing again. But *Friends* came to an end. He checked the time and said he needed to be going as he had football training that night. We kissed some more and he arranged to pick me up the following evening, Tuesday, for the supper thing at 7pm.

I leaned against the door after I closed it and could feel myself grinning like a Cheshire cat again.

Chapter 9

I was just about to go into the lounge to gather the plates and stuff when I glimpsed something that made my heart nearly stop. At the top of the stairs, there was a figure, sitting. It was dark at the top of the stairs so I could make out no more detail than that. I tried to let out a scream but like in dreams, no sound seemed to come out.

"Oh, don't panic," the figure said as she, for I could now see it was a girl, stood up on the top stairs.

"I'm not going to hurt you," she assured in a very matter of fact voice that implied it was her decision so I could rely on that.

She began to walk down the stairs. I guess my nervousness showed as I kept my hand on the handle to the outside door.

"It's OK, I said I'm not going to hurt you!" She had a very definite tone this time, kind of insisting that I believe her.

She reached the bottom of the stairs and sat down on the bottom step. As she was coming down, I could see her swollen stomach and in my head, I was putting two and two together.

"I'm Natalie," she said and before I could frame any question, she continued, "I needed somewhere to get out of this damned rain and Seb told me where you lived. I did go to the shed, but I must say, it was bloody freezing. I don't know how Seb stands it in there."

I sighed feeling like this afternoon was just never going to end.

"I expect you're probably hungry too?" I said eventually. I don't really know why, maybe in my head I had made associations between Seb and food, they certainly did go together. She nodded.

"Come on then, let's head through to the kitchen," I said in a resigned tone but her face brightened.

"Have you got anything hot?" I noticed how similar her face was to Seb's, very round and in some ways childlike, and when she smiled, it seemed to take over her whole face, just like Seb.

"Well, I'm not your 'masterchef' but I could probably do some pasta in a tomato sauce."

"Will it have onions in? I don't really like onions. I do eat them coz in some things, they are just too hard to pick out but I don't really like them."

"Well, usually it does…but how about pasta, baked beans, and cheese instead?"

"Sounds brill," she said with a smile and did a little clap of her hands.

I remembered about the stuff in the lounge so explained that I would just gather that stuff and suggested she took a seat in the kitchen.

I put the glasses and other stuff into the dishwasher and started opening beans and putting a pan of water on to boil.

Natalie was wandering around the kitchen opening and closing cupboards and then concentrating on the memo board in the kitchen and all the notes about dental appointments, dance classes, and bills to be paid, etc., just like Seb had done only a few hours earlier.

It suddenly occurred to me that I ought to ask how she had got in and of course, I figured that Josh hadn't been hearing things after all. She explained that as we tend to leave the key on the inside of the back door, she pointed to it then, it was easy. Relatively though she did say being heavily pregnant made it a bit harder, to lie on the floor and put your hand through the cat flap and turn the key.

"So when is the baby due?" I asked after her explanations of breaking (not really) and entering (definitely) were finished.

"Soon, I hope," she said rubbing her hands around her tummy and sort of sticking out even more, which she really didn't need to do as it seemed enormous to me anyway. She went back to her wanderings in the kitchen and then stood looking out of the French windows at the back.

"Someone said it was going to snow today. Its bloody freezing, that's for sure," she observed in a general fashion.

"Yeah, the sky looks really kind of heavy, doesn't it? So, I guess it might."

She turned around and smiled.

"Yeah, heavy like me, eh? Full of expectation you might say. Or full of baby in my case. Boy baby actually." She smiled broadly; I assumed she was smiling at her wit initially but then rubbed her tummy again and continued to smile, so maybe I thought to myself she was smiling about her baby. Which struck me as strange.

She was a teenager, 15 I think, single if you discount, which on so many levels it sounded like you should, the violent, drug abusing, jealous ex, and she had no parents, well no available parents with a dead mother and a father in the clink.

There was a lot of silence but I was OK with that coz I was cooking and she seemed quite happy just wandering round and asking the odd question.

"I'm thinking of calling him Isaac," she stated after a while.

"Nice name," I said nodding.

She was still by the French doors but had turned facing the kitchen as I put bowls on the breakfast bar. I noticed she took down her hood and looked at her reflection in the French window as she fiddled with her hair.

"Well, it might be simple but it's ready," I said.

She sat down at the breakfast bar and I remember noticing that it must have been hard to eat as she couldn't really get anywhere near the 'bar' because of her tummy. She managed though, wolfing the food eagerly and grabbing a spoon from the cutlery drawer (she must have noticed where I got things from I thought absently to myself), which she chose to use rather than the fork I had laid out for her.

Towards the end, she chased baked beans around the rim of her bowl, like naughty children determined to make an escape.

I drank the last of my drink and burped. "Oops! Sorry!" I said putting my hand to my mouth and feeling slightly embarrassed.

She put down her spoon having finished or given up the chase with the last few 'escapees' and grinned then let out the most enormous burp, it would have made a rugby player on a drinking binge proud.

"That's OK," she said.

I giggled a bit and then had to try and do something bigger than my pathetic real burp, so I did. Then she did another one, then we giggled again like a pair of silly 7 year olds.

"It says in the books that babies burp a lot," she said quite suddenly.

"Yeah, I think they do, not that I really know mind you. What's going to happen when you have the baby? Have you got somewhere to live?"

She just looked at me and then used her hand to move all the hair away from one side of her face.

"Oh my God," I said gasping at the massive bruise. "What happened?"

"Jay's what bloody well happened."

"He's your boyfriend? Did you report it? Is he the dad?"

"Oh, shut up for God's sake, you sound like a bloody social worker," she sounded assertive, almost cross.

"Sorry," I said. "It's just, well he can't, can he? Is it the first time?"

"No, it's not the first time. I know it's not right and I know you'll think why do I go back to him but you're not me, are you? You don't know what it's like. You have here your lovely cosy 'ideal home with a fucking Aga' life. Well, I don't and he's OK sometimes. Most times I suppose…"

Her tone had softened and then she just covered her face with her hands. I wondered if she was crying.

"It's just…" She started, having moved her hands away from her face, she sort of chewed the edge of her sweat shirt sleeve. "He can be so…nice! Do you know it's such a stupid word that, I can't believe I just fucking said that! Its like 'pleasant', stupid don't really mean anything. He was good, he was fun, he listened.

"When I first met him, years ago in another kids' home, I thought he was the only person who understood me. I remember telling him how I ended up in care and he told me his story and I remember thinking then that its only kids who it's happened to that can really understand what's its like. We got on well even then, but he was moved.

"That always happens; just get to know someone, doesn't matter if it's another kid, or staff or social worker, they seem to delight in pulling them away from you."

Natalie had become more animated as she spoke using her hands and her voice was getting louder.

"Seb didn't like him you know. Expect he told you?" I nodded.

"But he doesn't know everything, not really. Anyway when I met Jay again here, it was brilliant and we were older and well, things happened." She gestured to her swollen stomach.

"But then, he sort of changed. He'd been smoking a lot of stuff but you know…who doesn't—well you and your crowd I suppose *(I remember felling ashamed…why? Coz I had parents? Coz I didn't smoke dope? I knew plenty that did but I always just thought it was stupid! God! I am a bit bloody prissy, I thought to myself)*, but then he got onto crack then heroin, all in a really short space of time.

"He did start to change…a lot, I suppose, but only sometimes and he'd get really angry, jealous mostly, but then later he'd be lovely again. I think it was just the stuff."

She became quieter and nodded to herself as if to emphasise that this was true.

"So where is he now?" I asked as she paused.

"I don't know really. You see, I was going to try and move in with him. He had a place in a hostel and there seemed a chance we could get a place for us and the baby in another place run by the same group. But…"

"Is that a good plan do you think?" I spoke really quietly. I suppose I was scared she'd fly off the handle.

"Oh my God, well what do you fucking think? New baby, me, and a drug crazed psycho, right little happy family we'd be!"

She kind of spat the words out but then straight away was quiet again.

We sat for a few moments in silence.

"I know it's like what everyone says but really, honestly, it's not all his fault. He had a monumentally crap time growing up. His mum died when he was about 2, overdose I think, he found her apparently. He doesn't remember but he's been told. It's so important you know to do life story bloody work, rake over the past and if, mercifully, you don't remember some of the crap, then they bloody well tell you!

"Then his dad was hit by a drunk driver and killed outright about a year later. He then went to live with an aunt or someone, then she was diagnosed with cancer when he was about 6. So he started the round of foster carers. You see, not many people seem to want to adopt kids unless they're very little and very cute, and nowadays being from a third world country seems to help.

"I think he said he'd been to 8 different foster carers by the time he was 13, and then he was sent to children's homes, about 4 of them. I know it's still not right that he thumped me, or that he does drugs, but you have to admit, it's a far cry from your kind of cosy life, and far worse than any kid deserves.

"I mean it seems so basic, doesn't it? You have a kid, you love it and you look after it. You might get it a bit wrong but hell, who doesn't. It's a bit different from the kind of bad luck Jay had."

She sniffed and I noticed a tear was just poised to fall, like a diver on a board contemplating the drop unsure whether or not to let themselves tip over the edge. I didn't know what to do. I wanted to touch her hand or something but I thought she might shove me away.

I've thought about that since as it felt like a long time we sat there, though I know it probably wasn't, probably just a few minutes really, but what I think I was most bothered about was whether I'd be embarrassed if I tried to comfort her and she pushed me away. Pathetic really.

"I do really want to be a good mum, well at least an OK mum so I know Jay can never really be near the baby, and that will be another hurt for him. But he can't be, can he? Not till he's like proper sorted—but when on earth will that be? Can't risk it, can I? He just shoots up, loses it, and the poor little mite, might get it. My social worker is really scared that I'll move in with Jay and get into drugs and stuff; she must think I'm mental."

She paused again but I couldn't really think of anything helpful to say. I remember thinking to myself that I hadn't got a clue, not a clue about the kind of life some young folk have, and how pathetic it is to sit safe in a school as one of the 'bright' one's doing A levels and talking about statistics. Natalie was definitely not a statistic.

She looked young and vulnerable and it seemed she had no one who really could support her. I was *there* but I didn't have a clue. So I just sat there.

"Before, I mean before I got pregnant, Seb and me had planned to get a place together. I suppose that might work. I could get a flat probably after the baby, then maybe when he leaves care, but that is another 2 or 3 years away yet, he could move in too…and help out a bit, he is its uncle. Mind you…" She smiled, "he can be a right fucking eejit at times."

I smiled too as I answered, "Yeah, he said that he really wanted to move in with you. I think he'd been looking forward to it, in the future you know."

Natalie's phone vibrated in her pocket. She got it out and glanced at the screen.

"No prizes, it's Jay. Wondering where I am. He is constantly convinced that I've got some other boyfriend. My social worker is called Chris (a woman Chris as it happens) and he grabbed my phone the other day and went off on one saying who's Chris and who's Seb. I mean he's met Seb for fuck's sake but it's in his head that I won't stay with him long and I'll take the baby away from him…and he's right basically, poor bugger.

"I mean I'm not going leave him for any other bloke— chance would be a fine thing eh—right catch I'd be at the moment. But I will leave him. I have to leave him. It doesn't seem fair on him but I have to for the baby, don't I?"

"Well, if he hits you at the moment then he can't be safe with a baby, can he? So what are you going to do? I mean now, tonight?"

"I thought maybe I'd phone Chris, my social worker. She's a dozy old cow really but at least she can help me get a place I suppose. I mean I have a place at the home in Sharnbrook but they wanted to get me a place in a mother and baby hostel but I was all 'billy big bollocks' you know, don't worry about me I'll be OK with Jay."

She shook her head and sort of tutted at herself before continuing.

"As for where I'm going to go tonight, don't fret yourself, darling. Different world. It doesn't always phase me if I don't know exactly what's happening. Not like you in your pretty picture life with your dentist appointments and your ballet lessons." She said this matter of factly, not with any particular sense of malice, but sort of gestured with her eyes towards the memo board then she put her hand on her tummy.

"Oh," she said, "look at him. He's wriggling big time. Do you want to feel him?"

She grabbed my hand before I had the chance to nod.

With my hand on tummy, which felt oddly intimate and uncomfortable, I felt him. It was definitely a real kick. I smiled at her. I couldn't help as it seemed really exciting. I had simply not come across pregnant people.

"Sometimes he goes on all night. I swear he's a Jack fucking Grealish Feel that." She moved my hand up to the top of her 'bump'.

"That's his bum, heads right down apparently. He's a big bugger I think. God, that makes me scared. Only a few weeks and he's going to be coming out…ouch."

"Well, you know what they say if it were so terrible, no woman would ever have more than one." Was I really saying that? Miss philosophical midwife all of a sudden.

"Yeah, true say, not that many folk stop at one, nearly everyone has 2 or 3 or more even."

"Yeah, I guess so, apart from my folks. Well, I think they had another one, they don't talk about it much but I am the only one now."

"You poor bugger. May be you haven't got it all then!" She stood up and stretched arms above her head again, I noticed, just like Seb.

"Well, thanks for the pasta. Maybe see you again sometime, and thanks for being friendly with Seb. He needs friends, we all do I guess."

"Take care, Natalie," I said but she'd gone already out the back door, into the fast descending night her breath like fog hanging in the cold air behind her. I closed and locked the back door thought about taking the key out but decided against it. I don't really know why; maybe I didn't want mum and dad quizzing me because we had always, for as long as I can remember, left the key in the door.

I knew I needed to clear up the kitchen but I decided first to head into the lounge to get my phone.

Chapter 10

My phone was lying on the coffee table. I'd had a text from mum saying they'd be back about 8pm, about three texts from Josh saying…well nice things, and a text from Tess saying she'd try and call in about 7pm. I glanced at the clock it was 6pm already.

I headed back into the kitchen to start clearing up, happy just to be on my own for a few minutes. It seemed ages since Josh had been there and Tess had been really odd, couldn't fathom what on earth she was going on about, being all kind of cryptic and secretive. Half way though clearing up, I had a vague memory that I'd said to mum I would cook some grub for her and dad when they got in.

So I got some spuds ready and put them in the oven and started chopping an onion to do a veggie chilli. It was dark outside now and I checked I'd locked the door and this time, I took the key out of the lock and put it on the top of the fridge. I put on the lights and the radio, enjoying the cosiness of the kitchen.

Then I decided I would shut the blinds on the French windows, something we hardly ever did. I guess that's one of the effects of finding random teenagers in your shed and house.

I enjoyed busying about. When I'd got the chilli going and cleared up, I sent a text back to Josh, and wandered through to the lounge with a vague thought of putting on the TV. I sat on the sofa where I'd sat earlier with Josh. Could that really have been just a few hours ago? Somehow it felt like ages and as for being at school this morning, well it almost felt like another lifetime.

I had just got settled when the doorbell rang; it was Tess. I headed straight through to the kitchen with her, aware that if I got engrossed in a conversation in the lounge, I was bound to forget about the chilli.

She was talking all the way down the hall.

"Oh my God, I've been dying to talk to you since this morning. That's when I suddenly figured it out, this morning. It was last night I started thinking about it, you know putting it all together, I mean I wondered for a while, but only vaguely, I hadn't really worked it out. Till last night. Then of course, you left school before I could chat to you. Where were you first thing?

"If you slept in again, you're have to sort yourself out you know. Anyway, then there was first lesson then you went home, then Jack wanted to come round to get Josh coz they were working and I had to go back to school for Spanish…"

I interrupted her once we were sat at the breakfast bar in the kitchen I'd checked the chilli. It's not always easy interrupting Tess when she is on a roll, which clearly she was.

"What on earth are you on about? Your text just said you wanted to talk. I'm lost, Tess."

"Okay," she said taking a deep breath in and dramatically raising and lowering her hands in a calming yogic sort of gesture.

"I remember now I didn't put it in a text in case, you know, like that time I sent you the really sloppy text I'd meant for Jack."

I raised my eyes at her in a puzzled fashion as she was still being as clear as mud.

"I'm pregnant, Izzy!"

"Oh my God, Tess." I had to confess it was a shocker. Tess is always like massively organised and precise. She's the kind of girl who has everything from wet wipes to spare tights in her bag, she plans everything to the last detail and would be ooh soo unsympathetic to ANYONE who got themselves pregnant.

She also had an Irish catholic mother who was ferocious in a kind of rough diamond, salt of the earth, would help anyone one out, kind of way, but would somehow never approve of abortion, or probably sex before marriage. I made a mental note to be more appreciative of my own rather liberal parents. She also had four brothers, two older, two younger. I could see lots of valid reasons for a bit of panic.

"But I mean, how, when, weren't you on the pill?"

"How? Well, even Miss innocent Izzy knows that. When? I haven't a clue really but recently I guess, and yes, I am on the pill. So I don't know how really."

"Did you use condoms as well?" I put my Miss Crooks' face on. It was something she seemed to manage to get into every science lesson in year ten, not just biology but physics, and chemistry; any science lesson she'd somehow get that message in. Maybe she'd got an STD and wanted to make sure no one else ever did. She certainly had the zeal of a missionary; a sexually active, contraceptive protagonistic missionary.

"Yes, yes, we did," she said emphatically, then slightly more sheepishly. "Well, mostly anyway."

"My God, Tess, you make it sound like you were at it all the time. I don't know how you found enough opportunities."

"Trust me, Izzy, where there's a will, there's a way."

She smiled and then we both laughed, and then all of a sudden, she looked like she was going to cry.

"OK, OK, Tess. Look, how late are you?"

"Well, I wasn't very sure but then when I counted up, it's over 2 weeks!"

"OK, but that doesn't absolutely mean you are pregnant, there can be lots of other reasons."

"Yes, I know that's what I thought but then I woke up this morning and felt sick, and I've had to go to the loo a lot."

"Well, you could just feel sick coz you're stressed out about it? But you need to do a test coz if you are then you need to find out as soon as possible."

"I know…and I have bought one but I can't really face it, I'm just too scared."

"I know but let's face it, you are on the pill, you've used condoms 'mostly', so you would be really blooming unlucky, wouldn't you? But if you want to do it now while you're here, that's fine."

"I know and it would feel better doing with someone here. But I'm not sure. Can I have a hot chocolate while I think about it?"

"Course, babe, you can stay for tea if you like, it's chilli. I cooked it. Mum and dad will be home in about half an hour but they'll be fine with that, then we can shoot up to my room and we can do the test."

"Yeah, trust my Izzy to be the sensible girl. Hey, I guess we could do a bit of that sociology while we wait for your mum and dad?"

I pulled a face at her.

"Oh, talking of sociology, what on earth happened to you this morning? You'd think it was you with all the hormones, and what about Josh. Wasn't he the gentleman walking you home and everything."

I beamed at her.

"I know, he is just gorgeous. He was so sweet and attentive…and sensitive and lovely."

"Yeah, great abs too me thinks. Not that you'd be interested in that of course. A meeting of minds for you I should think."

"Well, at least I can't risk getting pregnant that way."

We both laughed and I sighed. I was going to spill everything out to my dear lovely Tess, about Josh and how I had decided I was going to sleep with him, pretty much as soon as I could, and about Seb and Natalie. I turned off the chilli, checked the potatoes, and sat back down.

"Well, shall I start with this morning…"

I was interrupted by a loud, "Hello, we got the earlier train. Oh hello, Tess darling. Mmm something smells good."

Before long, we were all sitting and eating dinner, chatting happily about all sorts of ordinary stuff, and I remember thinking just how normal it all was and how I had taken this kind of 'normality' so much for granted. Friends round, good food, parents who loved me and were interested in me and my friends, and were always happy to have them round. I suppose I just naively assumed that was how everyone grew up.

Yet at the same time, I know it wasn't, as I had grown up hearing mum's tales about the poor kids she worked with so I suppose the only way my feelings made sense was if I'd somehow not thought of those kids as real people in some way. Now of course, I could hardly deny that people like Seb and Natalie were real; they were far too real in lots of different ways.

Mum let me off clearing up which was usually a 'communal activity', because I'd cooked, so Tess and I went upstairs and I sent her straight to the bathroom to do her pee on a stick thing. I gave her strict instructions, obviously, not to dispose of said stick in bin. Call me a worrier but it was the sort of thing that would alarm your average, even if slightly liberal, mother.

She came back all smiles as it was negative. I did remember that I was going to tell her about Seb and Natalie but Tess is one of these people that sees each second of silence as a hole that she personally has a responsibility to fill. We did chat about Josh. She told me that she'd noticed on Facebook that he'd put he was 'in a relationship' with me, so we were officially a couple! I guessed that's why he said what he did as he left.

It really was no problem for me to talk about Josh. I could talk for England about Josh. In fact, the only thing that seemed better than talking about him was talking to him, and the only thing better than that was being with him and NOT talking. So because of the whole pregnancy near-miss thing, I asked her a bit about how she'd decided to and stuff.

Actually, we had quite a long discussion about sex—what it is, what counts. Tess told me that she'd read a book once where the woman was married and having an affair but she would only ever have oral sex with her lover as she somehow thought that wasn't proper cheating—well, we chatted about that quite a bit. She asked if I was going to have sex with Josh and I said yes defo and I couldn't wait really, which led to a conversation about where.

Her house is not often empty and she said she sort of wouldn't dare. She didn't agree with her mum's view but somehow to go there with Jack and shag even if they could ever find the house reliably empty just didn't seem right. But they went to Jack's sometimes—his older sister was at uni and both his folks were out at work mostly. I remembered then and asked her about the 'do' at Jack's folks' tomorrow.

She explained it was a pancake party—the fact that the next day was Shrove Tuesday had escaped me. But she said it would be fun and lots of the football crowd would be there, including probably Alex and probably Olivia because her family were apparently good mates with Jack's folks. She explained it was a kind of tradition that they always had folks around a cooked pancakes and it would be fun.

She pointed out, but she had no need to, believe me, that I would be there as officially Josh's girlfriend. Oh God, I suddenly thought of outfit crisis, so in the way of good girly mates, we threw open my wardrobe and started discussing outfits that would make me look hot—not sluttish, just hot. I said that Josh had said he and Olivia had parted on good terms but she said, and she insisted, I ought to be ready for Olivia in a 'you had your chance and you blew it' outfit for the benefit of Josh.

Then I got in a right panic about Josh's parents but she told me Jack had said they wouldn't be there because of some governors meeting or something.

When it was time for Tess to go, I decided to walk to the corner of the street with her. She lived just a couple of long streets away but if I walked to the corner and waited, she could walk along the next one, turn back and wave, and then she just had to walk to her house at the end of the next street. There was absolutely no need to do this but we'd always had to do it when we were little, mums' insisted as we each just had to walk on our own street on our own without the other one watching.

Quite what either of us would have done when smaller children if we'd seen the other be bundled into a car something I've no idea, but it seems parents construct lots of little 'safeguards' to prevent danger, which I guess makes them feel more secure even if the safeguards are woefully inadequate as a means of safeguarding. The fact is we always got to the other end of the journey, so maybe they were effective.

As I say, we tended not to bother these days but it meant I could have a few more minutes of chatting to Tess, mostly about Josh.

It was around 9pm when we left. As we walked up the street, we saw folks congregating at the top of the road waiting for the night shelter to open. I'd seen this sight a hundred times, more probably, in my head they were simply the homeless folk who needed a bed for the night. I'd never actually thought in a conscious way that it was their fault, but I guess somewhere in my head I thought that they must be responsible in some way for their plight.

I remember when I was little asking about it a lot, I suppose lots of parents would have been wary of living on the street with a night shelter at the top, but mum had always worked in some sort of social care and genuinely didn't feel threatened. In fact, our house had once been a hostel and when we first moved in (I don't remember this as I was only about 3 but I remember being told about it).

Folk would often knock at the door for a bed and dad would joke that it was all he could to stop mum asking them in to the spare room for the night before he could successfully direct them up the street to the shelter.

It was dark and snow was just starting to fall but not really settling very much. I'd just grabbed a hoodie but even just a few steps on from our house, I felt cold. The homeless folk were huddled together; I could see fags glow bright in their hands against the dark. That night, it was like I noticed each one as a real person, and thought about that for the first time.

Tess was still chattering away but I'd forgotten about chatting, I'd even forgotten about Josh; I was fascinated by the huddle. I wanted to go up and talk to them, find out each of their stories. I noticed one woman, she looked about 40, I suppose, and she had laddered tights and sandals on and I looked at my own feet in my Uggs and thought how freezing her toes must be. Tess and I had crossed to the other side of the road, force of habit, but I wanted to stare.

I felt not only fascinated but morbidly, magnetically attracted. How could I never have thought all these folk before, their stories their plights, their discomfort, the danger. There were several young lads with hoodies and one older man who was carrying an attaché case and seemed to be dressed in jaded suit trousers and an over coat.

He looked out of place but I noticed his coat was threadbare and the pocket was hanging off as he crossed the road to join another youngish bloke waiting away from the main group. Just as we reached the top of the street, the door to the house opened and they started to file in. Some with rucksacks, the one with the attaché case and a couple with sort of carrier bags, and some didn't seem to have anything.

There was a buzz of noise emanating from the group as we turned the corner where I was to stop. I couldn't resist looking at the group, and one of the young lads caught my eye. I wondered if it was Seb but told myself I was being stupid. I kind of tuned back in to Tess just as she was saying about it almost always better to wait till you felt like you couldn't wait any longer.

I know what she was on about, well I guessed it was some delayed feedback from our earlier conversation about sex and how you know when it is the right time, and love her to bits, but what a hypocrite! I couldn't resist commenting, "Excuse me, is this the girl who not an hour ago was peeing on a stick in my bathroom?"

"Exactly, learn from me and my mistakes."

"Err correct me if I'm wrong but learn what from you? You're NOT pregnant remember."

"Ooh I know. I still feel relieved and I know you never listen to me anyway and you'll do just what you want with Josh, which is right of course."

Tess hugged me as she left and I waited forcing myself to watch her retreating figure but I wanted to turn around and watch the group by the shelter. Tess waved when she reached the other end then disappeared round the corner. I headed back around the corner, back down to my house. Ahead I could see a couple of folk wandering away. I guess they hadn't got in tonight and I wondered where on earth they would go. It was still snowing.

I wondered how many homeless folk died from hypothermia. I almost felt cross with the shelter for not just letting everyone in. Surely it was better to be in a house on the floor than stuck outside on a park bench or wherever. But blaming the shelter was really missing the point. I wondered where Seb was tonight, and Natalie.

Maybe I should check the shed wasn't locked but mum and dad were in so they'd think it odd. I glanced at my phone at the time and realised Josh would be finishing training about now—it must have been indoors tonight, no underground heating on the pitch at their club. So, I planned to myself, I'd go in, jump in a really nice hot bath, then put my pj's on and ring him.

How on earth do homeless folk shower I wondered. None of them seemed to have very big bags, did the shelter give them towels I wondered.

As soon as I went in through the front door, I knew mum and dad had put the fire on in the lounge. It was a real fire and always gave of the most wonderful warm welcoming light, as well as real warmth of course. I remember when I was little, how mum and I would sit and watch TV with no lights on just the lovely glow of the fire.

Trying to toast crumpets on folks and always burning them a bit but eating them anyway with melted butter and jam running onto the plates.

They were watching some quiz show.

"Oh, Izzy, just in time. Who sang that umbrella song?" Mum called.

"Rihanna," I replied.

"Yes, yes, that's it!" It was dad this time. It was a 'lovely domestic scene' and it was comforting. The sight of them there, mum in her dressing gown enjoying a quiz show and a glass of wine by the fire. It was lovely and normal, and it warmed me just like the fire.

"I'm popping up for a bath," I said but I knew their attention was elsewhere.

I sent a text to Josh, well three actually as he replied back each time but basically, I said I'd call in about an hour after I'd had a nice long soak.

As I got undressed, I couldn't help thinking how odd it was that Natalie had probably been in here earlier, I found myself wondering if she'd touched my stuff, or taken anything, although nothing seemed obviously missing, but let's be honest, unless it was something like the bed or wardrobe, I'm not sure I'd notice other stuff.

Jewellery, for example, I wouldn't notice until next time I went to wear it and even then, I'd probably assume I'd left it somewhere else.

I put my favourite bubble bath in and luxuriated in the warm water. I could hear the TV from downstairs and bursts of laughter or a shout occasionally from mum and dad. I closed my eyes and slid under the water. I loved the way the sound became muted and muffled a bit like in a dream. That felt nice too.

Mum often told me how when I was little, I would pretend I was a diver and try to hold my breath for a really long time. I would make her count and try to stay under for longer each time.

Eventually, I got out and put on my dressing gown. I went downstairs into the lounge. Dad had gone into the kitchen so I sat on the sofa next to mum. She turned the TV off.

"So how's my best girl then?" She asked.

"She's fine, mummy bear."

She put her arm around me like she would always do when I was little.

"Listen, honey, you know you can always talk to me about anything, don't you?"

I nodded, part of me felt like crying again. It was just all so nice and I suppose I realised how really lucky I was.

"And I don't want you to think I'm a snoop but there was a receipt on the stairs and I looked at it just to make sure I could throw it out but I noticed it was for a clear blue pregnancy test. I hate to think you'd be worrying about anything without feeling you could tell me and I'd help you."

I smiled but I couldn't help feeling inwardly annoyed at Tess, she was so…scatty.

"It's OK, Mum, it was actually Tess', but in fact, it was negative. Good job she didn't do it in her house and drop the receipt, her mum would've gone ballistic!"

Mum smiled now. She knew Deidre and her reputation quite well.

"Yes, a calm reasoned approach to life is not what she's known for, is it? You're sure that's not just a 'my friend's got a problem' story."

"No, no, it really was her."

"As long as you know that there is absolutely nothing you can't tell me about. However bad it seems, there is always something that can be done."

"Is there, always? I mean do you really think that?"

"I do, honey, really. I don't think you can always make everything OK because life is full of consequences, but even in really tough situations, there are usually some choices and some actions that may make things better."

While she was speaking and I was sitting all snuggled up close to her, and she had this lovely smell that only your own mum ever has, I was thinking I would tell her about Seb and Natalie.

But then my phone started ringing in the pocket of my dressing gown. I was going to reject the call but mum said, "I expect you'll want to get that. Why don't we have a cosy girl's night in on Thursday? A Chinese takeaway and a DVD. It seems like ages since we've really had a chance to chat, and I'm working late tomorrow night and line dancing with your dad on Wednesday."

I nodded. "Sounds good…oh and I'm going to a pancake thing with Josh tomorrow night," I said as I headed out of the room answering my phone and blowing mum a kiss.

"Hi, babe," Josh said. "I didn't wake you, did I?"

"No, I was just chatting to my mum but I'm heading to bed now."

"You're taking me with you then I guess."

"Well, yea I am."

"God, what a pity I'm just a voice on the phone."

"Well, I'm shattered and it will be lovely to chat to you while I'm getting really sleepy."

"Just as well I'm only on the phone then, coz if I was in bed with you, I'm not sure I could let you sleep."

We chatted for ages and it was brilliant, and he arranged what time he'd collect me the next night for the do at Jack's house and then I suggested he came over to mine on Wednesday for tea coz I knew mum and dad were going out. I have to be honest, I was exhausted but if he'd walked in the room right then, sleep would have been the last thing on my mind too.

When we'd stopped talking, I drifted too happily to sleep, my mind full of Josh. I could still hardly believe I was actually going out with the gorgeous guy I'd fancied for so long.

Chapter 11

I'd fallen asleep with my thoughts full of Josh and I woke up just the same. I could tell as soon as I opened my eyes that it had kept on snowing through the night. There was that lovely light in the room that you only ever get after snow. I pulled back my curtain and the white blanket was deep, several inches. I got straight up realising I'd be better to walk than go on my bike so I'd need a bit more time to get ready.

Mum was on the phone re-arranging some appointments; the roads would be hopeless for a time. Then I had an awful thought, what if school was closed? Normally, I'd be really glad but the thought of not seeing Josh till later was awful. Even as I thought it, I told myself I was being really pathetic. Surely even if you are in love, it can't go on like this, feeling all the time that you simply can't be apart that; the most important thing in the world is being with them.

In my brain, I was scanning lots of soppy song lyrics that I'd scorned before and realised maybe they were true. Maybe this is how people feel when they are in love. I realised mum was talking to me.

"Hey, dreamy! I said they haven't put it on the internet yet but I wouldn't be surprised if schools are closed. I've got the local radio on so we may hear in a minute. But I suppose you ought to get ready anyway."

"Yeah, I was thinking I'd walk over and see what's going on. If it's open, I have got plenty of course work to do even if the lessons don't happen. Are you going to work?"

"Yes, but I'll leave a bit later and I've changed a few things around and actually what's left in my diary is all very local. In fact, if I get to the office, I could walk to a couple of visits from there. I hate driving in snow, it terrifies me really, so I might get your dad to give me a lift to the office. There's some toast there, love, if you want some."

I grabbed a slice of toast and spread it with peanut butter and poured myself some orange juice.

"Is it OK if Josh comes round tomorrow night for grub?" I asked remembering what we'd arranged last night on the phone.

"Of course, love, but it will be an early eat and nothing very grand coz we're going dancing." She smiled and wiggled her hips.

"Oh, I guess it might not be on," she continued. "Although, we can walk, but I suppose the teacher might not be able to. No, I think I remember her saying she lived quite close to the swimming pool."

"Well, I best get ready, let me know if you hear anything about the school." I'd started to head up stairs but I could hear mum calling so I stopped.

"Izzy, did you say you were out tonight at Jack's?"

"Yeah, that's the plan. Josh was gonna pick me up but I could walk, no problem."

I headed off upstairs, toast in hand. Josh had texted me to say he was going in to school, so had Tess. Weren't we all the really keen ones!

There's a lovely stillness that comes with snow. I walked out the back way into the lane. I could see footprints from birds and cats but thankfully, no human ones. I say thankfully but part of me wondered where Seb was. I hope in his home on a night like last night and goodness knew about Natalie. I did check the Wendy house as I passed but the door was shut and it didn't look like anyone had been in there.

I was walking along happily, admiring how pretty everywhere looked in the snow. I had my iPod on with my earphones in so I nearly jumped into next week when I felt a tap on my shoulder. I turned and saw Seb smiling.

"My God, Seb, you nearly gave me a heart attack," I said as I took my earphones out. "Don't tell me you slept out last night?"

"No, what do you think I am stupid or something." He was smiling as he said it!

"I crept out this morning. I don't know where Nat is. Did she come yesterday?"

"Yes, actually she did, and I felt really worried about her but you can't go giving my address to everyone, it's not a bed and breakfast…garden…you know!"

"Did she say where she was going?"

I thought back. "No, not really. She just wanted to keep out of Jay's way I think."

"That's why I came out. I know the places she often goes so I was going to check them out see if I can find her."

"And what then, what's your plan?"

He shrugged his shoulders. "A snowball fight probably." He laughed and had that lovely childlike grin.

"Oh, Seb! I didn't mean that! I mean what's she going to do? She's going to have the baby soon, she can't just sleep in outhouses."

"Well, Mary had Jesus in an effing stable!" He was still smiling.

"That's not real, Seb, and in case you haven't noticed," I said gesturing at the snow, "it's a bit chilly lately."

As we walked, he kicked at the snow sending it up in flurries.

"So are you going to school, won't it be shut?"

"Well, it might be I guess but they often open it for sixth form who want to study even if lessons are cancelled."

"So you got out of bed just to see; you must be a right geek."

"Yeah, I suppose I am but it's also fun, my friends are going."

"So you'll have snowball fights?"

"Yeah probably. Also," I lowered my voice a little but I really don't know why, "my boyfriend is going in today."

"I thought you said you didn't have one!"

"Well, we've only been going out for a few days but I've fancied him for ages."

"Well, don't end up like Nat."

"Don't worry I won't."

"How do you know? Are you a prude and you won't let him touch you?"

"No, I didn't say that but...well, we'd be careful...sensible you know."

"Course I know, I'm not stupid."

"Well," I said being all proper. "You're only 14 so you probably shouldn't!" The thing is, I had to look up at him as he was so tall, so we both laughed.

"Yeah, I keep forgetting I'm just a 'little boy'," he said smiling again and gesturing speech marks with his fingers around little boy, the way he did.

He bent down to pick up some snow and I could see he was making a snowball.

He turned and said he was going to go off down Lansdowne Road.

"That's not for me, is it?" I said looking at the snowball.

"Well, I am just a little boy." He made a playful face then headed off. I'd gone about 10 steps when I felt it hit the small of my back.

I turned smiling to myself and stuck two fingers up at him as he waved to me.

I remember one Sunday afternoon when grandma was round, it was before she moved into the nursing home. She had dementia, and I guess she had it then. She had come to stay with us for a few weeks after my granddad had died. She was very forgetful.

I could go out of the room to the toilet or to get a drink and when I came back, she'd be sort of surprised to see me, but she still seemed to know who we all were, most of the time, though she could never remember where anything was and she would often ask why she was at our house. I suppose because she had forgotten that her husband had died.

We would have to remind her that she was staying with us because Jim had died and it wouldn't be nice for on her own and she would sort of accept it. Her face would cloud over for a few minutes and then she'd just go on with whatever was happening at the time. I guess she'd forgotten again, till the next time she wondered why she wasn't at home.

Anyway, one Sunday afternoon, we'd been sorting through some of her photos and there was one of her and Jim, a really old black and white one outside a roller rink. I'd asked her about it and she told me how her sister had taken the photo with a box camera she'd won in a writing competition. It was one of the first 'dates' she'd been on with Jim.

She told me all about it and got up and showed me how they'd skate round arm in arm (she was 78 so not on skates obviously) and how Jim could go backwards and do twirls and was a bit of a show off. I remember how her eyes lit up and she was really animated.

Then she grabbed my hand with both of hers and said, "When you get moments like that, you've got to be sure to breathe them deep, then put them in a bottle and store them safely away in the loft in your mind. Then when you are old like me, you can just take one down and enjoy it again a little bit and remember how wonderful things were once in your life."

That was where mum had obviously got her whole bottled memories stuff from.

But grandma had been really sort of intense about it, I suppose that was why I remembered it. Well, that and the fact that mum had said it to me lots of times too.

Well, that day at school in the snow was one of those days; everything about it was brilliant.

Quite a few of us sixth formers were in but the younger years all got sent home. The few that hadn't heard the announcement on the radio that the school was closed and had made it in. Quite a lot of teachers were in, I guess they were marking or planning. There were no proper lessons and we did do some work but we chatted with each other a lot and had a few snowball fights, and laid down on the field and made snow angels.

Josh and I were together the whole day, others as well of course but it was like they were all out of focus and I was in this other dreamy snowy world just with Josh. We kissed a few times. At one point, Tess said to 'get a room for goodness sake' but it was like nothing else mattered apart from Josh. I just wanted to drink him in. I just couldn't get enough of him. I think I had a smile on my face the whole day.

In the afternoon, we went for a wander into town with Tess and quite a few of the others. I still felt in quite a dreamlike state. Josh and I always seemed to be quite a long way behind the others, chatting and holding hands. He kept telling me how beautiful I was, how he'd fancied me for so long, how he'd been really upset when he thought I must have another boyfriend but even then really loved me and didn't want to make things worse for me, and lots of other stuff about how he was really keen for us to sleep together.

He had this way of looking at me that made me turn to jelly. Honestly, rational sensible person that I am, if he'd suggested we jump of Prebend Street bridge into the river, I'd have probably done it. When he looked at me, especially just before he was going to kiss me, it was like his eyes saw right inside me.

I had thought of telling him all about Seb and Natalie but somehow everyone was kind of light-hearted and it seemed like a 'down' kind of topic, so I didn't. But not because I felt I couldn't. We talked quite sort of intimately about lots of personal stuff; well sex mostly I guess, our views and thoughts and well that is all pretty intimate.

I remember noticing I didn't feel at all shy talking about it which I often do, even with Tess who sometimes talks about little else. It just all felt very natural and right to be talking about it with him.

On Prenadine Street, there is a day centre for homeless folk. I had sort of always known it existed coz it's the sort of thing mum would mention to me, she had always been at pains to point out how lucky we were and how often it's not someone's 'fault' they end up on the streets. It's just so much more complicated than that.

I noticed watching my friends up ahead that they all crossed the road before they reached it, but to be fair, that might have been because there was a few folk gathered outside smoking and chatting, a bit too loudly. I guessed they'd been there for lunch, which was one of the things the centre did, provide a good nutritious lunch for not very much if anything, at all.

We crossed too and as we did, I noticed a young lad with his hood up. He turned and we caught each other's eye. I think it was Seb but I couldn't be sure.

We were all headed in the vague direction of Costa to have hot chocolates. We turned up one of the less salubrious side streets. The kind of street that you walk up if you are in a group but you'd avoid on your own and take a detour around if it was dark. Typical town centre but not re-developed and trendy yet.

Some kids were out messing about in the snow and just a few doors further on, there was a bloke sitting in a doorway sort of talking to himself. He looked very unkempt and as I walked by, I noticed he had that smell of BO and booze. I think he asked if we could spare some change but his speech was indistinct and slurred, and we just walked by. Further up the road, a woman came out of a house, nearly knocked me over actually.

She had bare legs and a really short skirt and cropped top; her long dark hair was really matted. Her shoes were bright and really high heeled but one heel was sort of bent over. It must have been a mission for her to walk in them at the best of times let alone run, which was what she was trying to do, in the snow! She ran past us in the direction of the day centre but I don't know if that was where she was going.

We had our hot chocolates then each of us set off to our own homes. Josh had agreed that my walking to Jack's with Tess was a good plan given the snow. So I walked towards home with Tess chatting about course work and of course our favourite topic of conversation, Jack and Josh. I saw mum's car outside the house as I approached and thought she was probably home but then remembered that she had planned not to drive it and looking at the snow still on the roof guessed that was the case.

I called as I went through the door. I think sort of hoping mum would be home. It would have been nice to just sit and chat to her a bit, mostly about how great Josh was I guess, and in fact it needn't have been mum. I think almost anyone I came across would have got their ears filled with the greatness of Josh. But no answer came so mum was obviously still at work.

I headed straight upstairs and took off my soggy clothes. Unusually, I put them straight in the wash bin, this was one of mum's usual nags that if I put laundry in the basket, and rubbish in the bin, my room would bear less of a resemblance to a cross between a jumble sale and land fill. I sort of moved things around the room a bit. I think that's what tidying is really but I had to say it didn't look too bad, in my opinion— not sure if it would be up to a 'mother' standard.

The steaming hot shower felt so so good. I hadn't realised how cold my feet were, but they gradually thawed in the steaming stream. I dried and put on carefully chosen matching underwear, just in case (in case of what I wasn't quite sure but I wanted to be ready I suppose for the moment when hopefully, Josh would see me in my scanties and hopefully, they would be sexy and matching rather than white, gone grey, and ancient).

I was just about to put on the outfit especially chosen by myself and Tess—so if needs be, I could outdo Olivia in her 'you had your chance and you blew it outfit', when my wardrobe door swung open. To say I nearly had a heart attack is an understatement. I think I screamed out loud—something I never manage in dreams when I feel under threat.

"For God's sake, woman, don't be so dramatic," said a disembodied voice from the wardrobe.

"It's only me! Natalie." But then Natalie or a mummified version of her appeared. She had her hood up and a big scarf right around most of her face.

I had the urge to fling something at her.

"For God's sake, woman!" I started sarcastically. "Stop being such a f...ing Ninja." I paused for breath.

"Oh and here's another thought," I continued almost surprised at my own anger but I guess it was just shock, my heart was still going like the clappers. "Stop breaking into to other people's houses." I was shouting by the end of the sentence. I grabbed my dressing gown. There is something disarming about having a row in underwear.

Natalie looked insulted and replied petulantly that she hadn't broken in.

"What, so you knocked at the door and mum said 'oh hello, young girl, I have never met you. Why not come in and wait in my daughter's wardrobe, then you can scare the living daylights out of her, that'll be a wheeze'. I don't think so somehow!"

She walked over to the bed.

"No! Actually, your dad was clearing the snow off his car and he'd left the front door open. I suppose he was going back in for something and I just seized the chance. I believe you call it optimistic!"

"Well, you could, but optimistic means looking on the bright side. I think the word you mean is opportunistic." I listened to myself English blooming teacher or what?

"Yeah well, that's what I said, innit?"

Natalie sat down on the bed and took down her hood and unwrapped the scarf she'd cocooned her face with.

"Oh my God, Natalie, what on earth happened?" Her face looked battered, both eyes swollen, her lip swollen and bleeding, and of course, still the bruise from yesterday.

"Jay."

"But, Natalie, we've got to get you to a hospital." She lay down on the bed, slipped her hand under the bed and pulled out an ice pack which she'd presumably been using before she heard me come in.

"No! It's OK. The swelling is going down a bit already and I've still got all my teeth." She tried smiling but looked like something from a horror movie.

"Have you seen Seb today?" She asked me.

"No, oh wait a minute, yes, yes, this morning. He was going to look for you he said."

"Oh God! That's just what I don't want."

"But wouldn't it be…sort of comforting to have someone you can trust at least not to hurt you?"

"If Seb sees me like this, there is no telling what he'll do. He'll know it was Jay, no matter what story I try to concoct and then he'll go looking for him, probably with a knife, or am f…ing gun or something. He's younger than me I know but he always tries to look out for me. God, what a mess!"

"Look, I do think you need to get yourself checked out. What if your nose is broken or something and the baby, what if he's hurt the baby?"

"No, he didn't. Actually, he usually does throw the odd body punch, but he just concentrated on my face. I think he wanted to make sure I was so ugly, I'd never get another boyfriend, did a decent job for the moment." She tried smiling again and I have to say, I smiled with her. I mean how could she smile?

She seemed so bloody lost yet so…resilient, like whatever crap this bloody life threw at her, she'd somehow find the funny side. I wanted to hug her, really I did. I just wanted to wrap her (and her swollen belly full of baby) up in my arms.

"Anyway, I have been 'checked out'," she continued. "I called into the day centre and the nurse there saw me. I told her 2 girls attacked me coz they thought I'd stolen some money from them. I know she didn't believe me and then she said she was going to phone, get me a taxi that is the sort of thing they'd normally do at Prenadine Street. They don't usually interfere massively but me being pregnant changes that I guess.

"I thought she was going to phone social services so I left through the other door and legged it. I saw you and your mates up ahead and I wanted to avoid you, so I headed up here. I'd had some grub at the centre so I just wanted to have somewhere warm and comfortable for a few hours, and thanks to your dad, I got it."

"Look, my mum'll be back soon and I know you don't like social workers but she would be able to help honestly."

I had sat down on the bed beside her. She sighed and took my hand.

"Look, you just don't understand. I want to have this baby and I really want to be a good mum. And I know now that Jay can't ever be with the baby or me. I don't really think it's all his fault but he is just too messed up to be normal."

She was quiet for a moment before continuing, "I'll go back to the home and explain that I never want to see Jay again and that I don't think he should ever get the chance of being with the baby, unless he gets himself properly sorted out you know, off all the drugs but also with some help for all the rage he seems to have in him. Ask them to move me somewhere a long way away from Bedford.

"I'll certainly get the sympathy vote at the moment. I mean, won't I?"

"But if you talked to my mum, she could give you a lift and help you out and stuff, explain what you want to your...care people, social workers, or whatever."

"I still have a tongue that works, I can do that, and I need to avoid Seb, then ring him and tell him where I'm going. Although, maybe it's better if he doesn't know in case Jay goes looking for me and finds Seb. You see, if your mum gets involved, there's procedures she'll need to follow and it will just make everything even more complicated. Honestly, I know you're wanting to help but it would make things worse."

She sighed again and looked so weary.

"Do you need to sleep for a bit or can I get you some food or anything?"

"My god, will you stop being such a bloody do gooder!" She sat up. "My life is just not like yours and you can't just fix everything easily."

She swung her legs off the bed and stood up.

"Look, can I not just give you the money for a taxi to get you back to your…home, you know where you're staying, where you should be I guess?"

"Yeah, if you want, it'll make you feel better, like you've helped, won't it. Like you've done something for a poor unfortunate."

"That's not the point, me feeling better. I do want to help but everything that I suggest, that I really think would help, you say 'no' to!"

"Like telling 'mummy'!" She did that gesturing speech Seb thing just like Seb does.

"Look, it isn't my fault I've still got a mum, I'm just lucky I suppose."

I rooted in my bag, got my purse, and gave her a tenner. She looked exhausted as well as battered. She wound the scarf around her face and put her hood up again. She moved towards me with slow steps.

"Don't want to be frightening the neighbours, do we?" She said as she checked in the mirror that the scarf obscured most of her battered face.

She took the tenner.

"Thanks though, and if you happen to see Seb, don't expect you will, don't say anything to him, will you?"

I shook my head. "I've got other plans tonight," I said, smiling.

"Oooh! Obviously, the boyfriend. Well, you looked fit in your undies so have fun. God I can hardly remember not having this flaming big bump. I can hardly see my own feet."

I went out the front door first just to check mum wasn't walking up the street, but she wasn't, so Natalie left. I offered to call her taxi but she said she would walk to the bus station and pick one up from there. I remembered then that mum had said she was working late.

It was already pretty dark must have been going on for 5pm. I went back inside and put on jeans, tight skinnies, that I always got compliments on, and a newish top, a leopard print blouse just like we'd planned. It was silky and baggy and came just to the top of my jeans; it had frills on the front and a low, but not too tarty, neckline.

Dad shouted up that he was home and I shouted back I was getting ready. I did my makeup and decided I'd have my hair down so straightened it. I headed downstairs. Pity was I had to cover this carefully planned outfit up with a duffle coat and wellies so I could walk with Tess to Jack's house.

Chapter 12

I must confess to being a bit nervous as I stood with Tess at the door to Jack's house. I knew Josh was already there as he had sent me a text—Tess and I had rather ambled our way there despite the cold, chatting, linking arms like we often did and had since we were kids. We'd chatted about school and our boyfriends, and I've wondered since but don't think I did at the time, why I hadn't told her about Seb and Natalie, but anyway I didn't.

Jack answered the door and invited us in, but Josh was close on his heels giving me a swift kiss as he helped take my coat. Introductions followed. Jack's parents knew Tess pretty well and knew me as her mate. They were very friendly. There must have been about 20 folk there, a mix of parents and kids from our years at school. A couple I didn't really know who weren't from our school but I guessed must have been part of the football crew.

Alex and Olivia were both there, so was Paul from sociology. There was lots of food and drinks laid out in one room and I gathered the tradition was that everyone tossed one pancake in the kitchen.

Jack's house was large; a double fronted version of ours and once we'd all done the regulation 'tossing', the group seemed to divide itself into parents and teenagers quite naturally, with the younger contingent taking over the lounge. Jack's iPod was attached to a docking station and we chatted and it was all very 'pleasant'. I was strictly drinking coke. I do like alcohol but once in a while is fine with me.

Quite a few of the boys were drinking beers from bottles but it was very relaxed and fun. At one point, Paul was sitting next to me and he said that he hadn't meant to cause upset the other day, though his eyes had a glint as he said it, but he thought the whole point of sociology was to debate and discuss. I certainly didn't intend to get into a discussion about Seb and Natalie with him so I agreed with him and said I hadn't been feeling well, and of course it wasn't him that upset me.

Paul is the kind of guy who I think would take it as a personal achievement if he thought he could upset you. I also chatted with Olivia briefly but politely. We'd never really been mates, she being a year above me, and she looked good in her skin tight pencil skirt and blouse.

But Josh had been so friendly and tactile and kind of protectively attentive to me, making sure I had a drink, food, tossing pancakes with me, staying nearby when I was chatting with Jack's folks that I didn't feel threatened by her for one second. I felt in fact that it was just lovely being Josh's girlfriend. At one point, I remember thinking how awful it would be to feel like that about someone and then have them change and hit you.

Not that there was any doubt in my mind—it had been absolutely instilled into me by mum (who I guess had seen at close hand just too often the consequences of an abusive relationship), that it only ever happened once, even just one

124

slap then the relationship was over. That seemed entirely logical to me. Tess and I had discussed it, and we'd had lessons about the general theme in both sociology and PSHE.

But I think what struck me was that I couldn't imagine how awful it would be if you really loved the guy. Like Natalie seemed to love Jay. Like I felt about Josh. I wondered to myself if I had felt like this about Alex. I didn't think I had. I mean we'd got on well and I thought he was fit but not the way I seemed to feel now about Josh. I could just look at him and my stomach did somersaults and my knees seemed to go weak.

He was really confident, all the time probably, but definitely in a comfort zone here and he was able to make folk laugh with some of his witty remarks and I felt very proud to be his girl. I think I'd decided already but I knew then that he would be the guy I'd sleep with. I just wanted it to be soon.

My musings were stopped a little when Josh got out his guitar and a few of us had a great time kind of busking through some well-known but slightly old numbers—Maroon 5, Coldplay, even Norah Jones, which seemed to summon the parents into the room, clearly not wanting to miss out. But it was school the next day so people started to leave.

Josh and Jack insisted on walking with Tess and me for the first few streets. There was absolutely no need but hey, we weren't complaining and it meant we could take the short cut down Foster Hill road by the old cemetery which was an unlit road that we wouldn't walk down on our own but seemed fine with two guys. Although, there was a full moon and no cloud, so with the white snow, it really wasn't too dark at all.

It also meant the chance for some 'kissing' stops along the way. I simply melted each time we kissed; the fact it was dark and freezing just faded into the distance when his warm soft lips were on mine, slightly beery but I just couldn't get enough.

All too soon we reached the parting of the ways. I checked Josh was OK for tea at ours the next night, arranged for him to come around at 6.30, reminded him I left school really sharpish as I had a dance lesson and then of course, kissed some more. Tess, I thought, was slightly tipsy. I had noticed that she'd had several glasses of wine (that was about the strongest thing on offer).

She put her arm through mine, a gesture of friendship rather than a need for support, she certainly wasn't drunk. But she had been plenty of times. She was my best friend but did have this slightly wild streak. I'm not sure if that was because of her strict parents or just a part of her personality.

She'd been on holiday with us several times and I remember on the first night when we'd gone to stay in the house of some friends of my folks in the south of France, she had drunk so much at our visit to the local bar (she had her own money and we'd gone without mum and dad, we'd been 15-16 but Tess had always looked, and acted older than her years), that she threw up in a ditch as we walked home.

She'd begged me not to tell mum but of course, I didn't need to, mum just knew. One time when she was staying over at ours and we'd been out at someone's party at a club in town, she'd cut her hand really badly. When we got back to mine, I woke mum up. Tess said it was fine and not to worry, but it seemed to keep bleeding through whatever we put on it and being a bit of a worry pants, but also knowing it wouldn't phase my mum, I got her to check it.

She bandaged it up properly but also said that she may need to go to the walk in centre the next day. Tess was in a right panic coz she hadn't told her mum that we were going out to this party, just that she was sleeping round mine. So she started constructing all these elaborate lies for her mum to explain how she got hurt on a broken bottle. In fact, I think my mum rang Deidre, who was none too impressed, and poor Tess had needed three stitches.

I remember the next day mum impressing on me that it was always safest to tell the truth. She gave me scary but accurate scenarios like if I told my mum I was staying at Tess' and she told her mum she was staying with me and then whatever plan we had went pear shaped, who could possibly keep us safe. Worry was often about keeping people safe, she'd often repeat to me. Parental worry nearly always was.

She also said it was hard and that she would no doubt get it wrong but she thought it best if I just told her anything and for me never to feel there was anything I couldn't tell her. She had even said then that she'd rather I came home if I was going to mess about with boy because she knew in my bedroom we'd be safer than parked in a car up some dark alley or hanging about in a park or something.

So I knew she'd be OK if Josh stayed over. I had tested it out a few times too. I once rang her at 3am in a tearful state, actually that seems to happen when I get really drunk. So probably that's why I'm pretty moderate. My friends told me not to be stupid and said she'd be furious, but she just came to collect me, dropped my other drunken mates off to their homes and then gave me a hug.

She made me drink a big tumbler of water, and left two paracetamols by my bed coz she said I'd need them when I woke up. Its funny how as kids we seem to think parents have been born middle aged but of course, as both mum and dad have told me on numerous occasions, they were young too once and, though times change a bit, I guess there is a lot of similarities about what young kids want to do.

This had all be going on in my head while Tess and I walked the few streets from where the boys left us to our parting point.

"Look!" She said pointing at the ground. "Moon shadows."

She was right and we spent just a few seconds making our shadows disappear by going back around the corner. Then she waited at the corner (we were going the opposite way this time) till I waved from the end of my street. As I left her, I wondered again why on earth I hadn't told mum about Seb and Natalie. I was sure she could help in some way.

There was no huddle at the homeless hostel now because it was later. The door was closed and I could see lights on through some of the windows. I guess the lucky ones had their beds for the night and the others well, where on earth would they go. I turned to wave then headed down to our house. The downstairs looked in darkness so I guessed they headed to bed.

I used my key and went in through the front door. There'd been a fire in the lounge which was glowing softly. I went through to the kitchen to make a cup of tea to take upstairs. I knew I had to sort out my dance stuff to take to school tomorrow so planned to drink it while I packed stuff up. I noticed the key was in the back door lock.

I took it out and put it back on top of the fridge, which was where it was supposed to go, we just all tended to be a bit lax about security.

I looked through the French windows at the back out into the garden. No sign of anyone in the Wendy house but I wasn't sure if I could tell really. I headed upstairs and mum shouted a 'goodnight, love' and I shouted back. When I got to my room, I actually did do a quick check in the wardrobe just to make sure there were no unexpected guests in there before starting to get organised for the next day.

But it didn't take long until I was snuggled up in my bed. To think I had spent my whole life grumbling about how cold our draughty old house can be in the winter, clearly I simply just didn't appreciate what I had. Maybe I was just a bit of spoilt 'mummy's girl', I thought as I drifted into sleep, comfortable and safe in my bed with loving, caring parents just along the corridor.

Chapter 13

I looked at the clock as soon as I woke up, it was 5am. I didn't know what on earth had woken me but I looked out of the window. The weather had changed completely; the sky was full of clouds, dark and foreboding, no sense of the earlier lightness from the moon which was so completely obscured, I could almost have thought I had dreamt it. It was pouring with rain.

I could see the snow was disappearing fast but of course, it still felt freezing cold, now with a depressing dampness.

I couldn't make out anything in the garden but I knew someone was in the Wendy house. I had a moment's thought of caution, like in a scary movie where the heroin decides to go alone into the basement, woods, loft, or whatever when all the audience knows that's where the serial killer is. But it was only a moment. I put on my dressing gown and Uggs and headed to the kitchen. I made Nutella sandwiches, hot chocolates, and grabbed 2 'sacksumas' from the fruit bowl.

Seb was there and took the hot chocolates from me as I bent to enter. He'd clearly been expecting me.

"You woke me, didn't you?" It suddenly became clear in my head this wasn't a sixth sense or some intuitive affinity for a fellow teenager.

He nodded and I went on, "Pebbles at the window? Like with Nat?"

I couldn't say I had consciously heard them but obviously something had woken me.

He nodded again already half way through the Nutella sandwich—I offered him mine too. He was reluctant at first but I said I'd eaten about 10 pancakes which wasn't too far from the truth.

I noticed his legs were in a sleeping bag.

"Getting equipped for the shed life, are you?"

"Well, you know…" he said through his sandwich.

"Stroke of luck really. I found it in a cupboard at the school up the road." He angled his head in the direction of the children's home.

"You mean the home?"

"Well, 'hactually'," he used his over pronunciation 'style' again.

"The building at the top of Wiston Lane, the school, it used to be the home then they moved us into a building on Maple Road *(he paused I supposed for effect as he had finished the sandwich now)* because that building… was… haunted!"

I nearly spat out the gulp of hot chocolate I'd just taken.

"What a load of old bull. I don't believe in ghosts."

"I don't believe in ghosts," he mimicked in a high pitched pretend girl voice.

"You would if you stayed there!"

Silence.

"Well, go on then. I've got to hear the 'story'," I said emphasising the word 'story'.

He shifted a bit and sat more upright, leaning forward slightly like he was a grown-up and I was a small child, he seemed able to do that, he cleared his throat and deepened his voice.

"Well, as you know it is a very old house. The tale is that in Victorian times, the house was lived in by a prominent businessman from the town. He apparently made his money in transport...horses and carts you know. He had all the contracts for transporting beer barrels from the brewers to the 'ostelries' in town. His wife was not in the best of health and they had one child, a boy who was 10 years old."

He paused to take a drink—I must say he had me hooked, he told a mean tale.

"Well, the tale goes that this man worked every hour God sent and the boy was home from boarding school for the holidays and was looking out from the gate for his dad coming home one day. He saw him and ran but didn't look before he ran into the road and was hit by a horse and cart...one of his dad's horse and carts.

"The horse reared up, hit him in the head *(he was using his hands now to embellish his tale telling),* then moved forward again but the cart unhitched...or something...and he was crushed by the falling barrels."

"Oh, that's really sad," I commented.

"Errhum!" He cleared his throat again.

"The tale does not end there..." He went on. "The father rushed to his aid but of course it was too late and the poor boy died. His wife struggled to come to terms with her grief and a short time later, threw herself from the attic window (that had been her son's playroom apparently) and died as she hit the ground. Though those what knew her said she'd died of a broken heart before she threw her body out of the window."

"God, that is sad!"

"Errhuum!"

"What? More?"

"The father couldn't come to terms with this double loss and fell to drinking. Then one night when he could take the grief no more *(he put his hand to his head in a dramatic gesture of grief and paused for effect again)*…he hung himself from the top staircase."

"Not a happy tale then!" I commented sarcastically.

"Yeah, but they are still there. Honest you hear them. That's why they made it the school so no one has to sleep there. But things happen. Doors open upstairs and staff would say you'd hear crying, either the boy or the mum from the attic room. And sometimes you'd hear glass chinking as the old geezer pours himself a drink in what used to be the parlour—I think it's the science room now."

"Really, you're not just pulling my leg?"

"No, honest, well I have never actually heard them but obviously, I'm never there on my own and the attic room is only used as a storage room now. But I know the 'school' staff hate being there on their own."

"So you live on Maple Road and go to the school in the building on the corner of Wiston?"

He nodded.

"How many go to the school?"

He used his fingers to count up.

"About 10; 5 from Maple Road and a couple from another kids home in Elston and a couple who live with foster carers but have been excluded from regular schools—yours probably."

"What's school like?"

"Well, better than yours I should think—some of the staff are OK—you get the odd one, you know who thinks they are all that but on the whole not bad. It's the other bloody kids that's the pain. But we have a lot of lessons with just a couple in the class. They take us out and stuff a lot, and I guess like anywhere, there are some what you gets on with better than others.

"My favourite teachers are Ricky, who does art, he's brilliant, and Bella who is Portuguese but she's soft as shite and lovely, sort of mumsy I suppose."

"Does Nat go to the same school?"

He shook his head.

"Probly meant to but Natty doesn't really do school, hasn't done for a long time."

"Were you here last night?"

"Nah, I went to bed like a good boy. I'd found this sleeping bag, in the attic of the school actually…and it is really creepy up there. I found a bin bag up there as well and so I put it in the bag and threw it out the window, then went down and hid it behind the bins. I was woken up by two of the other lads having a barny one had absconded and when he came back, he'd been drinking and started a row.

"Staff were all pretty busy making sure they didn't kill each other so it was pretty easy to slide out and get the bag and make my way to my other…'place'."

"Oh, and rouse a poor young girl from her beauty sleep?"

"Yeah, sorry about that coz, boy, do you need it!" He said this grinning at his joke.

His face changed suddenly.

"You seen Natty?" He asked.

I think she'd told me not to say—but I'd paused and even if I'd said no, I think he would have known I was lying. So I just nodded.

"I think she is probly avoiding me, which means she's probly seen Jay again, and he's probly hit her again?" He made a point of not pronouncing probly, properly.

I made a 'that's about the measure of it face'. But then said, "Look, I know you haven't much time for social workers but I am sure my mum could help."

He stretched and started to move.

"Nah! Thanks but nah, we'll work it all out somehow—kind of have to. Anyway, don't you have a bloody school to go to?"

He smiled as he said this and had a kind of tutting look like I was the wayward child.

"Yeah, yeah," I replied 'in role' as I stood and made my way out of the door while he carefully gathered his sleeping bag rolled it really small, put it in the bin bag, then stuffed it behind the bean bags that were already there.

"Guess you are planning another visit then?" I said light-heartedly but he was already doing his lumbering jog up the garden in the pouring rain.

I noticed that there was hardly any snow left as I went back in the house, rinsed the mugs and headed back upstairs. I checked my phone for the time and decided it was hardly worth going back to sleep but I couldn't resist getting back into bed just for the sheer warmth and comfort of it. Honestly, I wouldn't survive one night if I had to sleep in a shed in a garden, even with a sleeping bag.

Chapter 14

I don't know if I actually slept but I must have dozed a bit because my alarm startled me. I got dressed, ate a bowl of muesli, gathered my stuff and, as the snow had all but gone and it wasn't really raining much now, I decided to go on my bike. It would be useful to have it to get from school to my tap lesson and then home again as quickly as possible.

My dance class finished at 5.30 and Josh was coming at 6.30 so time was of the essence if I wanted to get home and shower and dress before he arrived.

School was pretty uneventful. We didn't have sociology so I wasn't in any lessons with Josh but we 'found' each other at lunch time in the common room. We chatted about the previous evening—he suggested that he could play his guitar later round at mine.

I said OK but, although, I loved dancing singing and performing, I suppose growing up in a house with a musician, much as that may have been what engendered my love of performance, I had spent far too many bored afternoons in random pubs on far too many Sundays to be able to enjoy too much impromptu music.

Our paths didn't cross at all in the afternoon as I left as soon as the bell went to get to my lesson. I changed and put up my hair and started the tap warm up. That what was I loved, the discipline of it. No wondering about what to do next—it was all 'scripted'. The steps of the warm up were followed by specific exercises.

When the teacher spoke, it was in a language I got. I didn't have to wonder, ever, what she meant. So the time went quickly and it was always really enjoyable, even though we worked hard. Jazz warm up began with some really tough routines that always made me breathless.

But soon it was 5.30 and I packed up my tap and jazz gear and pedalled home, through rain sadly. The house was empty, but no sooner had I headed upstairs than I heard mum shout that she was home and she went into the kitchen and started on tea while I showered, did my hair, got dressed, making sure first that I chose my underwear carefully.

I rummaged in my underwear drawer and chose a really nice bra and pants set, a kind of turquoise and black lace one which I'd bought at an Ann Summers' party. It was the older sister of a school friend who had Ann Summers' parties to earn cash while she was at uni. I understand it was her mum's idea; now that is what I'd call liberal parenting.

I checked my reflection in the mirror on the wardrobe in various 'underwear model' poses just to be sure. Before heading down to the kitchen to help mum, I made sure my bedroom was looking fairly tidy, at least with no soggy tissues, dirty pants or socks, etc., on the floor and I even made the bed look decent by shaking the quilt and carefully arranging my pink scatter cushions on top.

I had butterflies in my tummy and this awful feeling that he might not come for some reason. But when I checked my phone, I'd had some 'countdown' texts from him saying how he couldn't wait to see me this evening.

I gave a bit of hand in setting the table. Mum had done a goat cheese and tomato flan with some baked spuds and a salad. Mum said how nice I looked and that she was sure Josh would think the same. I busied myself about hoping she wouldn't feel the urge to have one of her embarrassing chats about safe sex or something.

Dad had arrived home and was in an irritating mood. He pretended to hate line dancing and go under duress but always on a Wednesday, he'd dance round the kitchen like a loon and mum and I both knew he loved it really; it had released his inner dancer!

The doorbell rang right on time and Josh was here. He kissed me in the hall. I took him down to the kitchen and it was all very relaxed. Within minutes, he and dad were having music and guitar chats which continued through quite a lot of tea.

We did a sort of joint effort on clearing up and stacking the dishwasher, then mum and dad, after a quick run upstairs to gather their line dancing gear, whatever that is, were off. Josh and I were still in the kitchen when we heard the front door shut. We looked at each other and smiled.

"Come on," I said. "Let's go in the lounge."

I headed up the hall, Josh following. I think part of me wanted to be sure that they really had gone. Dad could be a bit of a nutter and I wouldn't have put it past him to hide in the lounge just for a laugh. He'd certainly done that before when I'd had mates over, not boyfriends though. I shut the curtains in the lounge and put on the side lamp as it always gave a nicer, softer, sort of glow.

I then dashed into the hall because I just wanted to check the front door was really shut; it was. Josh was standing by the door of the lounge but I kind of zoomed past him as I suddenly thought I ought to check the back door. I called out to him what I was doing. I guess all the unexpected 'guests' who'd be dropping round had rattled me after all. When I came back up the hall, Josh was still there stood against the side of the lounge door.

"So are you planning to run around the house like a whirling dervish all evening?"

I stopped by him at the door of the lounge and he straight away drew me into his arms. We kissed and he put his hand at the back of my neck and in my hair. He pulled away for just a moment.

"Gosh, I don't think I ever realised your hair was this long. You should wear it down more often, it's gorgeous!"

He smiled and then kissed me again. I sort of leaned against him and he had his back to the door jamb. I felt one of his hands go under my top and touch the skin of my back. His touch was like an electric current and we kissed more urgently, then he was kissing my neck and my ear, and I honestly thought my knees might buckle.

I dared to let my hands wander to his hips and then I suggested we actually go into the lounge and sit on the sofa, unless he'd prefer to stand. He whispered softly into my ear that anywhere was fine as long as he could keep kissing me. I wondered do I let him know I'm on the pill; do I ask if he has a condom? But I smiled and nodded and grabbed his hand and led him to the sofa.

My heart was racing, partly with excitement and anticipation, but I guess I did feel a bit nervous too. I guess part of me felt a bit embarrassed that I was still a virgin, but I don't really know why.

We kissed and 'canoodled' on the sofa, then I sort of suggested that we might want to go upstairs. I suppose I wanted him to know that I was happy to, wanting to, in fact fairly desperate to, have sex with him. He said fine and we made our way upstairs. I was unsure how to let him know, short of saying it, that I was grown up enough to want sex, so when we got to my room, I loosened my top and took it off.

I guess part of me wanted him to see my carefully planned under outfit. I'd seen movies where girls did that too. He took his shirt off. I loosened the button on my jeans and then we were in each other's arms again. It was so lovely touching his skin, his back, his chest. He slid his hands in the loosened waist of my jeans and eased then down. I loosened his and did the same. As we each stepped out of them, he mouthed to me again was I sure and I just kissed him.

I still had my underwear on and he his boxers and we kissed again and moved towards the bed. Then there was this noise. Like a door banging. We both pulled apart.

"Did you hear that too?" He said. I nodded. We were both silent except for our breathing which seemed really loud. It was all quiet, but I could feel my heart racing.

I think we were both hoping we could it ignore it so we were just still and quiet for a few moments, hoping for it just to go away so we could get back to each other but then there was another noise.

"Should we go check it out?" He said but even as he said it, he kissed me and I sooo didn't want to stop what we're doing right then.

"No, probably just the wind, or our cat," I said, sort of hopefully but even as we started kissing again, we heard the unmistakable sound of footsteps in the down stairs hall.

"Shit," I said as I dragged myself off the bed and grabbed my dressing gown.

Josh got up too and pulled on his jeans. "Do you think they've forgotten something?" He said.

Josh managed to get ahead of me out onto the landing but I was just behind him.

"Shit," he said. We could both see a cross young lad coming towards us. I knew him to be Seb but Josh presumably thought he was a burglar.

"Seb," I called out. "What on earth is the matter?" Josh stopped but sort of filled the landing. Seb went right up to him.

"Move," said Seb.

He then put his arms up to Josh's shoulders to shove him. I could see Josh tense and brace himself as Seb shoved him roughly.

"It's OK, Josh," I said as I squeezed past. "Look! Seb! Calm down, let's go have a drink or something."

"You mean you know him?" Josh sounded really puzzled, in fact I think he was even scratching his head which made me sort of want to laugh, out of nervous tension I suppose.

"Well! Yes," I said as I started to head downstairs chatting to Seb as I went.

"Where is Nat? Have you seen her? Have you heard what he did?"

"Didn't you lock the back door?" This was Josh.

"Yes, but it sort of does no good," I replied to the Josh question about the door.

"No, I haven't seen her since yesterday, and I thought you knew what he did," I replied to Seb's question.

"Fucking hell, Izzy, I knew he hit her but what I'd heard was he slapped her face not that he knocked seven bells out of her," Seb shouted quite loudly.

I realised he must have been a day behind in our earlier shed conversation.

Josh now raised his voice too. "Will someone tell me what the hell is going on?"

"Look! Guys," I raised my voice as well. "Let's all go downstairs and calm down a bit and I can explain."

We went to the kitchen. I led the way and I heard Josh ask how Seb had got in if the door was locked, and Seb, calmly but like he was talking to a young child or a really simple person, that if you lay down on the floor, you can fit your arm through the cat flap and reach up and turn the key, if it's in the door, which to be honest ours always was.

Until the last few days, I'd taken to removing it but I guess knowing I wasn't going to be on my own, I hadn't been so careful. At least they were talking in normal voices and some of the 'heat' seemed to have gone out the situation.

"OK," I said when we'd reached the kitchen.

"Josh, are you OK to get some drinks and I'll explain to Seb what I know about Nat."

"Nice to meet you, Seb," Josh said with a kind of sarcastic tone. I motioned for Seb to sit down at the breakfast bar.

"You have seen her today?"

I nodded. "Hot chocolates, Josh, if that's OK."

"Of course, Madam!" He replied with a slightly camp intonation. He had managed to grab his jeans and put them on but he was still bare chested and maybe it's to my shame, but

I remember thinking if we ever lived in the same place, I would simply insist that he didn't wear a shirt; his torso was sooo sexy.

"No, it was yesterday, actually maybe even the day before. Yes, she looked pretty rough… but I thought you knew this morning, you seemed to know he'd battered her."

Seb seemed to ignore my comment and banged his fist on the table angrily, making me jump and Josh look round.

"I'll kill that bastard when I get my hands on him," he said through gritted teeth.

"Look, I know it's not right but I was thinking that in a way I think it has made Natalie see that she absolutely can't have a future with him and the baby simply won't be safe with him anywhere near it."

Josh glanced over with a 'what the hell is going on' hand gesture at the word baby, but I sort of shook my head and he went back to his hot chocolate making.

Seb was quiet for a moment and he somehow looked very young, head sort of bowed. For a moment I thought he may have been going to cry.

I was about to put my hand out to his but Josh came and put down the hot chocolates and drew up a seat. He smiled at me briefly but it was enough to say 'it's OK, I might not have a clue what is going on, but it's OK!'

It seemed to break the spell. Seb looked up, grunted a 'thanks', and took a slurp.

"Where was she going? Did she say?"

"Well, she said she was going to go back to the home and get them to call her social worker and…" quick slurp of hot choc for me. "…discuss the future. She could see she'd probably be better off away from here."

Seb banged the table again. "But then I won't be near her. It has taken me ages to get placed near her. She always messes things up, it was all her stupid fault anyway."

We were all silent for a few moments.

"Look," Josh said. "I know I don't know the story but it's obvious there's some pretty serious stuff going on. Do you think it would be worth talking to someone, you know… official?"

Seb looked at him, his eyes widening, and for a second, I thought he was going to get angry or at least bang the table again but he just took another slurp and shook his head and rolled his eyes at me towards Josh as if saying 'he doesn't know the half, does he'.

"Can't really trust them, well not to do what you think they should. Honestly I know, I've had enough flaming social workers and busy bodying 'professionals' who ALL think they know much better than me…about me. Laughable really!"

We all seemed to sit in silence for a moment, slurping our drinks and then Seb seemed to clock the fact that Josh was half dressed and I was in my dressing gown.

"Sorry!" He said with a smirk. "Did I 'interrupt' something?" He used his finger speech marks on the word interrupt.

I was just looking at Josh and partly remembering what he had interrupted and wondering how to reply when the doorbell rang on the front door.

"Who on earth can that be?" I said as I got up and headed down the hall. As I was leaving the kitchen, I asked Seb, "How did you know mum and dad weren't here?"

"Deerhhh? Watched them leave then waited for a bit," I heard him reply and I could imagine his expression, the 'you're so bloody smart but you know nothing' look.

I could see through the glass in the door before I opened it the shape of a hooded young person and knew it was Natalie.

"Is he here?" She asked as the door opened. I nodded and we walked down the hall.

I think I probably expected some sort of touching reunion but Seb, if anything, seemed cross at her.

"My God, he had a right go at you this time, didn't he?" Seb said as she took down her hood and unwrapped the scarf. Josh looked at me but I just sort of motioned to him to keep quiet.

"Nice to see you too, little bro," came Natalie's reply.

"What are you doing here anyway? She said *(Seb inclined his head to me)* that you were going back to your place and seeing your social worker?"

"I was, I did, but then I got a text from Ashleigh saying she'd seen you and you were looking for Jay, so I thought I'd better come and find you before you do anything really stupid. Ashleigh also mentioned that someone had told you he'd had a right go at me—who told you? Was it her?" She nodded her bruised battered head towards me.

"No, it bloody wasn't—but she should have done—well she knew I knew about the thump the other day but how on earth did you get near enough to him to let him do it again. He might have bloody killed you. It was only tonight when I ran into Dale that I realised he'd done more than the other day, so I told Dale I'd bloody have the stupid fucking twat."

Natalie looked utterly weary and I'm sure she must have been in pain.

Josh caught my eye and held up a cup, kind of asking if he should make another hot chocolate. I nodded. Nat had sat down at the breakfast bar and she looked just terrible. I put my hand on her shoulder as I sat down, next to her and she smiled a weary worn out smile.

"Are you OK?" I asked gently.

"Been better." She smiled her twisted battered smile, her face looked even more swollen.

Josh put down a mug of chocolate in front of her.

"Thanks," she said instinctively wrapping her hands around the mug. "I'm guessing you must be 'lover boy'?"

"Well, you know I was hoping!" Seb and Natalie smiled at his sort of joke.

"I left his place after he'd hit me—I saw you, didn't I?" She looked at me and I nodded and tried to work out in my head which day that had been. The last few days had passed in a hazy blur feeling head over heels in love and suddenly having these new, interesting young folk making an appearance in my otherwise, ordered existence. It really feels like my life was turned upside down.

"I knew I had to keep away from him but I'd left a couple of things I wanted at his place so I waited till I knew he was out and went in to get them. But he came back while I was in there, think he said he'd forgotten his phone. Of course, he knew what I was doing and he said if I left him, he'd never see the baby, which of course is right and he sort of lost it— but he never hit me bump."

"Oh, what a fucking gentleman he is!" Seb said matter of factly.

"God, you know I ache all over, me back, me bump, me head. I just feel shite."

"Do you want to have a bit of a lie down?"

"Nah, but thanks. I just want little bro here to convince me he'll leave well alone and not do anything stupid. Ashleigh said you'd talked about a knife."

"Ashleigh's talking a load of bull! I never fucking seen Ashleigh." Seb did his smile that made him look like a little boy, like he'd been found out in some way.

"But it's a plan eh?" He said, then held up his hands to her in a gesture of surrender. "But I haven't, moron."

"Watch it, fuckwit. I could still clip you round the ear."

Josh and I were very much on the side lines through these exchanges but I saw Josh smiling at this, because Seb was so enormous next to Natalie and she was so obviously battered and hugely pregnant. It was clear whose side anyone's money would be on.

"How'd you see Ashleigh anyway?" Seb asked Natalie.

"I didn't but I did happen to call into Prenadine Street, and you know what a load of old gossips they are there!" She answered.

"Yeah, and when I went there," Seb continued, "it was all a bit of a buzz talking about you and the 'fight' *(he used his fingers in the air to Seb commas again)* you'd had with some girls. I said girls my arse and that Jay had gone too far this time and that I maybe ought to pay him a visit sometime AFTER I'd called to see my old mate, Jed."

"Did you go to Jed's?" Natalie asked, looking alarmed while Josh and I just watched trying to make some kind of sense of it all. I remember thinking there were far too many boys' names that began with J. For goodness sake, there are other letters in the alphabet.

"No! Idiot, I'm not completely stupid. I wouldn't need a knife anyway. Jay's a pathetic coked up weed head. I could knock his lights out easy just with me hands."

"Jed?" I asked with a 'I just want to make sure I am keeping up' kind of face.

"He's got a reputation for tooling folk up."

Natalie stood up and sort of rocked and bent over.

"God, I feel rough and I keep on getting these pains in my back," she said.

"I'm no expert but I remember my sister said when she had my nephew that most of her pain was in her back. When is it due? Do you think you could be having it?"

It was Josh who had said this. I knew his older sister had a baby but it was a surprise that he seemed to know what was going on. I felt sort of proud of him; how many teenage boys would know that? Natalie was breathing in a really concentrated way.

"Shit something's happening anyway." She had stood up and now she leaned over to rest her head on her arms on the breakfast bar.

Josh sort of rubbed her back. She didn't object, she seemed to be concentrating really hard on something, breathing I think, and she made kind of moany noises.

"I think maybe you need to get to hospital or at least get checked out by someone."

I looked in my dressing gown pocket but realised that my phone was probably still upstairs.

"I'll go get my phone," I said.

"Just use the house phone there, Izzy!"

"God, I think I need to go to the loo," Nat said. Then there was this sound of trickling water. "Oh my God!"

"It's just your waters breaking. I think it means the baby is definitely coming, so, Izzy, you need to phone an ambulance and, Seb, could you get some towels and move a chair behind Nat."

Seb was opening drawers and eventually found a drawer full of tea towels which he handed to Josh.

"Oh God, that is just gross," Seb said.

"Could you get a chair for Nat from the other room, Seb?"

Josh seemed to have somehow taken complete control of the situation.

"Izzy!" I looked over to Josh when he shouted my name. I guess I'd somehow been in a bit of a daze. "You were going to phone!"

"Oh…yes," I said but I had just put my hand on the phone when the back door burst open.

A thin, wiry young man burst in, he looked 'wired' like he was high or something. I heard Nat say 'Oh God' but I wasn't sure if this was in response to the new addition to our 'party', who I guessed was Jay, or the pain she was obviously experiencing.

He put his hands into the pocket of his hoodie after putting his hands behind him to close and lock the back door he had just burst in through. I remember thinking absently that after Seb had come in, even though we'd discussed his unorthodox entry thorough the back door, none of us had actually thought about locking it.

Seb was stood behind the breakfast bar, Josh was standing next to Nat and he had one hand on her back and was holding her other hand. Nat had slumped onto the chair Seb had put behind her when Josh had asked him to and I was stood a little way behind the breakfast bar by the phone on the wall.

"Oh very cosy I see. I suppose YOU are the new boyfriend then," Jay said looking at Josh.

"As a matter of fact, no, I'm going out with…" Josh started to reply very calmly but Natalie interrupted.

"God, Jay, you just never listen, do you?" Then she went back to 'breathing' sort of in time with Josh.

"My God, you still don't fucking get it, do you?" Seb said this as he banged his fist down onto the breakfast bar. "She fucking loved you, you fucking twat, and look what you've done to her. She looks like a fucking boxer. Oh but yeah one difference, she's having a fucking baby."

Seb was spitting the words out. Jay sneered at him.

"In fact, I was just going to call for an ambulance," I said as I picked up the receiver again.

Within seconds, Jay was right by me, having legged it behind Nat and Josh right up close to my face. I could smell his breath as he put the receiver down, it smelled of tobacco and alcohol and sort of fruity too.

"We'll leave that a minute I think," he said with a sarcastic sugary sort of tone like he was talking to a silly small child.

Seb was standing quite near and moved closer to Jay in a sort of menacing way.

"Says who exactly, you! You little runt, I don't think so! Not man enough for a real fight, are you, just have to pick on girls, don't you?"

"Don't worry, 'little bro'. I just want a few words with Nat and then I'll be on me way!"

He moved really quickly again to stand behind Nat and he bent down so his mouth was right next to her ear.

"Go on, darling, you can be honest with me. Is this your new fella then?"

"Fuck off, Jay. I haven't got a new fucking fella, as I kept on telling you," she said this is gasps as she was trying to breathe or groan or something.

Jay straightened up and took a step back.

"Jay! Look, I know we've not met but honest, I've only met Nat tonight. But she is in labour right now and we need to get her to a hospital before this baby is born on the kitchen floor." Josh sounded really calm and a bit like a negotiator in one of those hostage movies.

Jay stood up and turned his back to them. He was right next to the Aga with his back to the rest of us and for what seemed like several minutes, but was probably only about 10 seconds we were all quiet, apart from Nat who seemed to be breathing louder all the time.

Then Jay turned round and quick as a flash, without any warning at all, he kind of threw a knife, a pocket knife I think right at Josh from about a metre away. It landed in his shoulder. I think I screamed. Josh sort of crumpled to the floor still somehow holding Nat's hand. Before he had hit the floor, blood was leaking onto his chest. He had no top on and it was just sort of running down his skin.

I remember Seb moving, I remember it quite clearly coz it was all in some weird kind of slow motion. He picked up a knife from the knife block at the end of the breakfast bar and went towards Jay. I remember shouting, "Noooo!" as I saw him raise the knife and plunge it towards Jay, who moved and grabbed Seb's hand and they tussled.

Then suddenly, Jay bent forwards and Seb stepped out and I saw the knife sticking out of Jay's abdomen. I remember thinking that mum would never be wanting to chop onions or carve anything with that knife again.

I stood frozen to the spot.

Nat was saying, "Fucking hell, Seb, what the fuck have you done…"

Jay was on the floor silent. Then Seb bent over and pulled the knife out of Jayson, almost as if that could make it all alright. I remember hearing Josh say weakly, "No, Seb, leave it in."

Josh was till slumped on the floor by Nat holding hands with her, the knife in him sticking out his chest and blood pooling on the floor as it dripped down his chest.

Jay lay on the floor with a fountain of blood spurting up from his body, through his clothes.

I think I was in some kind of stupor or trance for a few minutes, possibly just seconds, then I heard Josh's voice, shaky, "Izzy, Izzy, the phone, we need help."

"Seb, we need to stop the bleeding." It was Josh talking to Seb but he dumped the knife in the sink and ran out through the back door.

I remember precisely I was telling the 999 lady our address and I noticed as he left that it seemed to be snowing again, which seemed strange to me after a day of rain. Funny the thoughts that go through your head.

I put the phone down. Nat was sort of groaning and bent almost double. I could see beads of sweat on Josh's forehead which I remember thinking was strange as the draft from the back door was so icy, but he was shaking too and I remembered shock, and thought about cups of tea.

"Izzy," he was saying, "stop him bleeding." He sort of pointed with his head to Jay.

I looked blank and stood like a lemon.

"Get a towel or something, Izzy, and press on the wound."

"Oh OK," I said and grabbed the hand towel off the holder on the wall near the sink. I knelt on the floor by Jay. I put the towel where I thought the knife had gone in but it sort of sank into a pool of blood.

I looked at Josh.

"Another one, Izzy, get another one." I ran out of the kitchen to get one from the cloakroom then put that on top of the other one. It took longer but blood soaked through it again.

"I'll get another one," I said and set off to get some more but as I ran up the hall, I could see a blue flashing light through the front door. I opened it and kind of pointed to the kitchen.

I followed them into the kitchen. There were two initially but within seconds, they were radioing and it seemed the kitchen was swarming with paramedics and then police. In no time, a team seemed to gather around Jay and there were drips and bags and tubes, and then he was put on a stretcher and taken through the hall. Josh was put on a stretcher too and I noticed as he passed me that he looked a really odd colour.

Natalie too was taken in a wheelchair out to one of the ambulances; she was holding a mask over her face and seemed to be doing her concentrated breathing.

It was all like I was in a dream. I could see it all happening but felt kind of out of it. At some point, I sat down and I remember someone taking my pulse. When she took my arm, I remember noticing my hands. They were covered in blood. Jay's blood.

I asked if they were going to be OK. She said she thought it might be best if I came to the hospital too and they could check me out. I said I was fine but she said it would be easier if we were all in the same place, and the police would need to talk to me, and the others as soon as they could. I remember her muttering about contacting relatives and how I could probably help with that. I nodded.

Then I sought of passively followed her. My mind was racing about how mum and dad would need to get in the house but she said we'd call them and that policemen would be in the house for a while.

It had just started to snow again as I climbed into the police car and was taken to the hospital. Someone had put a blanket around my shoulders, a policewoman I think. I remember she had a lovely, warm sort of smile and I wondered if she had children. I remember thinking as I sat in the car that it must be a nightmare being a policewoman with children as you must just worry so very much.

Chapter 15

I don't know what time in the evening it was but I remember finding myself in a brightly lit hospital waiting room. There was lots of bustling going on around me.

I chatted, quite casually really, to a youngish female police officer, not the mumsy one who had accompanied me and got me checked in. I gave her a brief run through of what had happened. She said I would have to make a formal statement later.

I gave her names and numbers. She gave me a hot chocolate from the machine. Several times I asked about the others but she said the medics would be out soon enough to talk to me.

I remember seeing mum and dad walk through these double swing doors. I felt overwhelmed with relief. They came right up to me and hugged me. I cried, not the sobbing shoulder heaving kind of cry, just tears streaming down my face like some washer was broken on a tap that couldn't be turned off. I felt a bit broken although physically I was the one who was unscathed.

I buried myself into mum's shoulder and I could hear dad talking to the young policewoman. I guess we all sort of sat down, and mum gave me a hankie and dad went and got coffees from the machine for him and mum.

They, mum and dad, never really asked me, well not then anyway, to explain everything but someone must have filled them in a bit because at one point, I noticed dad wasn't there and she said he'd gone to check on Josh and chat to his folks. Police were around, generally. Mum said that when I felt up to it, I need to go through everything with them but she said she didn't think there was too much of a rush.

Mum was still drinking her coffee when one of the policeman pointed me out to a nurse. She came straight over and introduced herself as Mina in that bright breezy way nurses have.

"Hi, are you Izzy?" She said and both mum and I nodded.

"Hi, I'm Mina and I'm with Natalie and she said if you were still here, she wondered if you'd go and see her."

I think I was on my feet already.

"Yeah of course, has she had it?"

"No, not yet, but she's doing really well. She's about 8cm dilated already so probably only another couple of hours. I'm hoping she'll have him before I go off duty."

I realised I was walking off with her without mum. I stopped and turned round.

"Would it be OK if mum came too?"

"Well, she can come with us to the maternity unit then I'll have to ask Nat."

Mum sort of nodded that it was OK and started walking with us. She had a quick word with the policeman, who I realised was probably having to watch me, presumably so he could tell dad where we were.

"Have you known Nat long then?"

"No! About 2 days actually but it's kind of a long story."

"Well, we called her social worker but not sure what time she'll get here and you can't beat a familiar face when you're in labour. She's doing really well, she seems to know just what she wants. I offered her some pethidine when she first came in but she said she wanted it as natural as possible and she seems to be coping with just the gas and air at the moment."

We stopped outside a room.

"Izzy, we'll go in and if your mum just waits here a second, we'll see what Nat thinks."

Mina pushed open the door.

"Izzy, whatever she wants is fine with me," mum called to me.

I turned round and mouthed 'thanks'.

Natalie said it was fine for my mum to come in even if she was a bloody social worker—she reckoned I'd be little use but it was nice to have a familiar face.

I'd never seen a baby been born—it really was amazing. Mum cried but was really useful, and she and Nat seemed to get on great. Mina, the midwife, stayed longer than her shift coz she wanted to see the baby be born. It did seem to take a heck of a long time and I gathered later that it was actually quite a quick birth—blimey some must be serious mission births!

Also, it did seem like really hard work, lots of puffing and panting and a bit of screaming—it did look like it hurt like hell as well. He was lovely, when he did eventually appear, quite small given how enormous her tummy had been. 6lbs 8oz they said, three and a bit bags of sugar! Amazing really.

Natalie's social worker, Chris, arrived and wanted to know who I was, etc. etc., but by the time she came, Nat and mum were well into the whole birth thing, so the social work just sort of hung around in the room.

I remember at one point, after the baby was born, I had wanted to go and see Josh but dad said he was in surgery and suggested it was best if we went home and got some sleep. So we did. I had a long hot bath. Mum made bacon sandwiches and she never asked even one question, which I think must have taken a hell of a lot of restraint.

After I had got into bed, she came up and sat on my bed. I kept being tearful and she just hugged me and said there was plenty of time to make sense of it all but what I needed to do now was just sleep, if I could. Police would be around later and Natalie wanted us to visit her, and of course, we'd have to go back to the hospital to see Josh.

I sort of suddenly remembered Seb. Did anyone know where he was? She said she didn't know but we could leave all that to the police and social workers.

I think I did sleep. It had been one heck of a week. But I slept, warm and comfortable, in my bed knowing that whatever happened, mum and dad would help sort things out. I remember trying to work out where Seb might be—I didn't think he'd be in our garden at all, but sleep covered me like a heavy cloak and my eyes closed and my mind, thankfully, went black.

Epilogue

So that's it. That's what happened one week in one winter. Five days in one cold February. It is amazing how just a few days can change your life. Change so many people's lives. But then, that is how it happens. All the time, people's lives change in an instant.

You walk out into the road without looking. You win the lottery. You get diagnosed with something awful. Someone you love dies. Lots of people say that when you fall in love, life changes. I heard on the news the other day about a fire on cruise ship and some people died, others were injured; they hadn't bargained on that had they? They just wanted a holiday.

Immediately, after it all, I was a bit of a wreck—emotionally, not like Jay and Josh who were both wrecks physically and took quite a bit of putting back together, but at least, unlike Humpty Dumpty, they could be put back together.

It was quite a busy time. I had to give lots of statements and talk to all kinds of folk. It was 'news' of course, locally at least, and there were quite a lot of phone calls from folk wanting to talk to me, but mum and dad fielded most of them.

I think school was full of gossip. I wasn't there for a while, just couldn't face it.

But Tess did say when I saw her that Josh and I were all people talked about in the sixth form common room. Lots of wrong stories got out at first. Josh had been into drugs and hadn't paid his dealer, the house was broken into. My jealous ex (secret ex) who was a thug attacked Josh—you could imagine a few of your own and they probably would all have made an appearance in one of the hushed conversations in the corridors or common rooms.

It was, I think immediately after that, I started to feel guilty. It did really feel as if an awful thing had happened and it was entirely my fault. I know I didn't actually plunge a blade into either Josh or Jay and I know I never hit Natalie. But they were all congregated in my kitchen because of me. If I had told someone about Seb when I'd first seen him or about Natalie, then quite simply they wouldn't have all ended up with Josh and me in the kitchen.

When I mentioned that bit to mum, she said the same confrontation would have happened somewhere else, but would it? Jay lost it coz he thought Josh (naked from waist up at the time) was Natalie's new boyfriend. Maybe he wouldn't have thought that if Josh hadn't been there for the 'confrontation'. And he had presumably seen Natalie at my place sometime and maybe thought that was where her new boyfriend lived?

But I suppose, if he'd found Natalie when no one else was there, maybe he'd have really done for her, or maybe not if he wasn't jealous? Who can possibly know?

No one else tried to make me feel guilty, that bit was all me. I did that all on my own. My mum was brilliant, dad too, but as usual, he did his background thing. Like when I was little and he would push me around in the deep end of a pool on holiday, on a blow up boat or inflatable dolphin or crocodile or whatever, and he'd look like he was just floating but beneath the surface, he was kicking, he was propelling with his legs.

He was making sure there was forward movement, so that I would have fun and of course, always making sure that I was safe. So he did a lot of domestic stuff coz mum was doing other stuff. Mum never once told me off or spoke sternly too me. In fact, there was one point when I wished she would. I wanted someone to tell me I'd been a stupid little girl and look at what I'd done.

Then punish me somehow—ground me, fine me. Make me do community service…something to make me feel like I had paid some kind of debt. But of course, mum didn't punish me, neither did anyone else, though I could probably bet that Josh's parents thought it, even if they never expressed it, apart from maybe secretly to one another to comfort themselves as they lay in bed in the dark with their poor boy lying in hospital.

Of course, I told mum how I felt, but she said that there was just no point trying to apportion blame. I also tried to have a few 'what if' conversations with her too, but she said that wasn't worth it really. What happened, happened for all sorts of different reasons and all sorts of different factors were involved—if just one thing had been different, then yes the outcome might have been different but we would never know.

We reminisced about the film *Sliding Doors* with Gwyneth Paltrow, a real 'what if' fest.

Blame is normal and I suppose what I can see now, is that at least in part, I blamed myself because I simply couldn't make blame stick to anyone else. If I was looking for someone to blame, I guess Jay is prime candidate. But somehow I couldn't—he was obviously hurt, high, damaged, and paranoid, and a whole host of other things too. Seb could also be in the 'blame frame' but he was really just a kid.

I know that, legally at least, that doesn't mean you can't be blamed but it seems reasonable to me that he took the only action he felt he could to stop his sister, effectively his only family being hurt, possibly killed by Jay. Which is an important point really. If Seb hadn't plunged that kitchen knife deep into Jay just exactly when he did, what would the outcome have been?

Maybe we'd all be dead. Maybe there would be no cute little Jayson, or maybe he wouldn't have a mum.

One of my family's mantras has always been that in every situation, however awful, there is something positive that you can take from it. Hmmmm. I guess lots of folk would disagree. Anyway, in this scenario, I must say I never saw a baby been born and other than my own, hopefully some day in the future (totally different viewpoint then I guess), I don't know when I ever would have, but I must say it is marvellous, amazing; I simply couldn't get over it.

One minute there was Natalie on the bed groaning and panting and making all sorts of strange noises, and then literally within minutes, there was this completely separate little person. With hands and toes and a perfect little mouth, and a flash of dark hair, matted and plastered to his head, but a totally separate, brand new, little person.

Natalie wanted me to hold him, so I did, when he'd been sort of checked and wrapped in a blanket, and after she'd held him of course. She called him Jayson Isaac, which seemed kind of appropriate.

Natalie stayed in hospital for a few days. I visited her the next day and the one after, with mum. For all she was an 'effing' social worker, Natalie actually got on OK with my mum. Mum, of course, seemed to get on OK with Chris, the social worker, and the other social worker—little Jayson was given his own social worker—seemed crazy to me.

The night of the day after, the night it happened, after I'd been in bed for ages having a 'no sleep' (because I had slept for hours during the day), that's what we used to jokingly call sleepovers when I was little because of course when you first started going to mates for a sleepover, that's just what they were, 'no-sleep-overs', mum had insisted that I at least went to bed for a bit.

I slept deeply and for hours but I got up about 5. It was dark by then and we headed to Mothercare on retail park and bought some baby grows and a rattle for Jayson and mum bought a nice set of pyjamas and a dressing gown for Natalie. Natalie was awake and eating her hospital meal with little Jayson next to her in one of those see through Perspex cots. He was asleep but every so often, he'd sort of stretch out his hands or screw up his face.

Natalie was so smiley; her face was still lopsided when she smiled but she was chuffed—new mother chuffed I guess and the swelling on her face seemed a bit less but it was getting all multi-coloured now like a horrible gone wrong tattoo with a sickly yellow tinge.

She got a place in a mother and baby hostel just by the train station. I didn't even know that's what it was, another big old building, I hope that one isn't haunted. I went with mum a few times to see her and Jayson there but I haven't seen her for ages, since the day in court with Seb. Mum still goes and sees her sometimes and I think Natalie must be OK with that coz mum wouldn't go if she felt she was being a pain.

Jay was in hospital for a long time. That first night, he'd been to theatre and I think they said he was in intensive care but I remember Natalie saying she wanted Jay to see his son. I suppose she did when he was awake before she left the hospital. He couldn't be a risk to anyone then, too many tubes and drips. His case went to court first. I think he'd had a fair number of run-ins with the police and he got a 'custodial', he actually was taken away to prison.

He looked a bit better by the time he was in court I think it was around May, he wasn't so thin. All pretty horrible, he had no family of course, just his social worker and his youth offending team worker, his drug worker, and a psychologist who'd been doing some 'therapy' with him (maybe for him, on him, to him…not sure). I thought *how sad*, all those people and no one that was actually related.

No one who would stick around and not leave him for a promotion or a because the case got 'reallocated', or because they wanted to live somewhere different or do something different with someone else that they really cared about. I just can't imagine that it must be just so awful.

Seb was missing for a number of weeks. I know mum and dad kept checking the Wendy house. They actually had a better lock fitted to the back door—higher up so even a gorilla would have trouble reaching through the cat flap for the key. I don't know where he went or what he did or why. But I'd hazard a guess that he thought he might have killed Jay so was scared to come back.

He's reasonably OK at finding places to sleep and I know he thought he was streetwise, but there was this big kid side to him that Natalie, wise for her 15 years, thought would make him vulnerable. It was still really cold and I did worry that he could easily die of hypothermia. It was an awful thought.

He must have been so lonely and though he'd never admit it, scared about what might happen, about Natalie and the baby, maybe about being found and charged and going to prison.

Anyway, he did come back. Mum let me know he was safe and back at his care home. He didn't come back to sleep in the Wendy house as far as I know, as in I didn't actually see him, but one day when the weather was warmer and the sun was actually shining, I came through the back garden and the door to the Wendy house was wedged open with a 'sacksuma'. It made me smile.

I looked in of course but there was no note or anything and no Seb, but I was left smiling. I liked Seb, I really did, and I think he was partly like a kid brother. I don't know of course coz I've never had one, although when I spoke to mum about it once, she said the baby she'd lost was a boy and he would have been about Seb's age. Maybe, although I don't remember it, it left a kind of brother shaped hole in me somewhere that Seb somehow seemed to 'fit'.

There was a court session with him too of course, and his was a lot more serious in many ways coz Jay really did nearly die. But Seb was younger, didn't have much previous cases, shop lifting and stuff but nothing serious, and of course he acted in defence. He could see Natalie and knew he had to do something and he did.

It's so easy I think to blame people for what they do when you haven't been in that position. Easy to say 'well I'd have done this, or that and never been so stupid', but you never know really, you can't, no one, whatever they say, can see into the future. Even their own future because it can all change in a whisper; just one or two chance happenings can change the whole course of things.

He was given a supervision order and had to attend special sessions each week. Natalie and the baby came to court too and Seb, well he was just lovely with Jayson. I think he gets to see Natalie and Jayson quite regularly. His social worker kept calling him 'Uncle Seb' and he'd tell her to stop but you could see he liked it.

He even spoke to my mum; he saw her holding Jayson at one point and I think he must have the view that if Natalie thought mum was OK, then she couldn't be completely awful even if she was an 'effing' social worker. I suppose my mum must be a pretty good social worker. She has certainly stayed in the same place a long time—maybe that could be a rule for social workers, that they have to stick around with the kids, but it would never work, I can see that.

Mum seems good just at getting on with teenagers, and she seems able to make them smile and stuff, so even when they start out thinking they aren't going to like her, and I get that coz she is an idle aged, middle class, white woman, so on the surface not much in common with lots of the teenagers she must come across, they do.

But lots of social workers do that and the kids like them and maybe even get to rely on them, but then of course, they go coz at the end of the day, it is just a job to them. Which it is and I can see that their own lives and families must come first I suppose. But it's life for the kids. It's their childhood, the only one they will ever have. I hope they get some 'bottle' moments but I bet they are few and far between.

And let's be honest, if you have got a social worker, then you deserve a bucket load of special bottle moments because something has gone wrong somewhere to mean that they have a social worker anyway. And if they don't get those with whoever looks after them, how can they ever end up being good parents for their kids?

I still think a lot about this sort of stuff. I haven't got all the answers but I definitely think there is a lot wrong with the way things are at the moment.

I didn't see much of Josh. That night at the hospital after the baby was born, I knew he was having an operation. I wanted to go and see him but dad said better not. The next night, when we'd gone back to see Natalie, I said I wanted to go but mum said his parents were there so maybe we'd better not. But we stayed with Natalie for quite a while and then mum surprised me by saying why didn't we check and see if they were still there.

They weren't, and the nurse said it was OK so I went up to his bed. His eyes were closed, his arm was right over his chest, all bandaged and he had a drip in the other arm. I touched his arm, the one with the drip and he opened his eyes and smiled. That lovely smile. A sleepy, dopey smile, but lovely.

"Quite a night?" He said.

I nodded.

"They said it'll be a few weeks till I'm back at school," he said.

I nodded again. I was truly lost for words. I think I muttered 'sorry', then I think I started to cry and mum came into the room and chatted to Josh a bit and then took me home.

I didn't see him for ages—he wasn't in court because he had exams—special dispensation and he was a victim, he hadn't done anything wrong, well apart from go out with me. He gave statements and testimony and everything because he was a witness as well.

He missed quite a chunk of his last bit of school and then come May was on study leave. We texted each other a few times, and kind of agreed that if we saw each other at school, we'd be 'distantly polite'. It just felt like we'd be in this kind of glare with folk watching us. But it only happened a couple of times and of course, he then left and is just about to start uni at Warwick.

In July, after school was closed for holidays, he texted me and asked if I fancied meeting up somewhere for a drink. I thought maybe he wanted some sort of 'closure'; got that from my counsellor. But we did and it was lovely. I think we'd both been laying low so hadn't even run across each other at social do's—and there'd been exams and everything.

Then as soon as exams were over, I had to go back to school to start my year thirteen. I also had several dance exams and I have to say, no disrespect to my counsellor, but dancing was really kind of calming and therapeutic. It was like I just could switch off my brain and put all my energy into my dancing.

I'm not recommending it as an alternative therapy (though why not there are stranger ones out there I am sure), but all those hours I danced to escape the racing thoughts in my brain paid off. I got distinction in ballet, tap, and contemporary (amazing), and a merit in jazz. My AS results were pretty good too, though largely I think down to coursework, which I'd already done by the time all the craziness happened.

Oh, and I passed my driving test—I have been busy. Josh did well too. He got an A and 2 Bs, very impressive…but then he is. Often when I thought back to that night, he really was amazing. He kept calm, knew just what to do, and was just brilliant.

So we met up for a drink and we did talk about that night. I think I tried to explain why I hadn't said anything to him about Seb and Natalie but he had a what's-done-is-done attitude. A kind one, not like when teachers say it when kids are apologising but they are going to give you detention anyway—hasn't happened to me much but I've seen it.

I told him about my dancing, I asked about his shoulder— all normal stuff. He said I wasn't really flavour of the month—year even—with his parents but he also said that he thought we'd both needed a bit of space, and we had exams. He said at one point that he thought if we'd seen each other, we would just have ended up going over and over stuff.

We chatted quite a lot about uni and he asked if I still liked him. I told him I did. I also told him that I'd been seeing a counsellor (why? was it not blatantly obvious to him I was a nutcase anyway!) and that she suggested I write the whole thing down. He thought that was a good plan.

Then he said how about me going up to see him at Warwick when he got settled, fresh place, etc. etc. Well, I said yes. In fact, I was maybe a bit too eager. I think I said, "Yeah that sounds good. Yeah, yeah, great plan, yeah." And I probably nodded too.

Then he kissed me as we said goodbye.

So I wrote down my story and gave it to my counsellor, like homework, and I said that I didn't think I needed to see her anymore. Which I guess is success for her; I guess I go in the ticked column. It has changed me, I am definitely not the same as I was. I still have fun, go to occasional parties, but I also have a kind of heaviness inside.

Sometimes when I do have fun, I feel sort of guilty, which I gather from my counsellor is what happens when people grieve after someone they love has died, or they've lost something, a baby or a limb, maybe. But actually, I didn't really lose anything, except perhaps the last bits of carefree childhood. But heck, I was 17 and lots of folk have no childhood to speak of at all.

I guess really it was naivety I lost. I realised that not everyone has parents able to love them the way parents should, for all sorts of reasons. I learned I guess that life is jolly tough for some folk and simply not at all fair. But hopefully, I would have figured that out at some point anyway. I guess I lost Josh for a while but hopefully not forever.

Yesterday, I had a text from him (we text almost every day now, sometimes more) saying how about next weekend, could I borrow mum's car and drive up to see him.

Mum is fine about the car, so I can, and I will.

And I can't wait; roll on, next weekend!